The Promise

Victoria Southard

ISBN: 9780615972251
ISBN-13:

DEDICATION

I dedicate this book to my family who has
always stood with me !

CONTENTS

The Promise

Chapter 1

England 1640, Black looked around the clearing to assess the damage. All seven of his men are accounted for with only scrapes and bruises to report. He gave the order to set up camp and clear the bodies. All was quiet in the small clearing; the only noise was the pond rippling as Black looked to make sure all was secured. He gave orders to have the bodies of the bandits removed and hauled off far from camp. "Give them the burial they deserve," he said as he spat on the ground. The bandits he was talking about what the Grouch Gang, he and his men have been looking for, for almost a year. They came upon them strictly by accident while on their way home to take a much needed break from policing the Queens lands. They put up a good fight but in the end none were left standing. The Queens orders were to locate and allocate the bandits to stop their thieving and killing. They had also been known to take a maiden or two for their pleasures and then disposing of their used up lifeless bodies along the road.

It was a lucky break to come across them especially when they were completely unaware of their presence. Black was a man with many years of experience in chasing and tracking down the bandits. He was commissioned by the queen to police her lands for the low lives that plagued the country. He is very dedicated to his role as peace keeper knowing all too well the tragedies that lay in the path of these men, the destruction of lives that are ill replaceable. Black himself was orphaned at ten along with his young sister Mary who was only three at the time. His parents were traveling to court on summer afternoon when they were attacked by highway men, but they didn't just rob the couple they murdered them, in cold blood, now Black believes it's his mission in life to rid his country of these men.

Raised by his Aunt the Duchess of Sacks who had no children of her own but was well off financially. She was a mutual type person not much motherly kindness in her. She was however kind to Black and Mary and when Black turned of age she allowed them to return to their home and Mary became his ward. The Duchess however would check up on them from time to time, for all her hard exterior she loved the two of them and wished for nothing but the best for them.

Black however made it his life's ambition to align himself against the evils he believed were crawling across the land. He and his little band of men combed the country side in search of these bandits, to dispose of, arrest or bring to justice the filth of the world.

As the men who were left in camp brought fire wood and watered the horses they all started to gather around the fire to catch some much needed rest. Black had run them into the ground on the hunt for this band of men. Now they are all disposed of, bodies dragged off to a far off area to be taken care by the animals, which Black thought was more then they deserved. A little talking and some food were being prepared on the fire when

Richard one of Blacks men heard what he thought was a chain rattle. As he listened for the sound again he noticed that the others didn't seem to hear it. When the sound didn't come again he went back to eating his bland dinner. Soon as night fell the men all sprawled out on their blankets, resting their heads on their arms and as one kept watch they slipped off to pleasant slumber.

Richard was first watch. After a few hours he became tired of sitting and started to stealthily walk the perimeter of the small field. As he perched himself on a tall stump he saw Black approach to take the next watch. Just as Black arrived they both heard an almost in audible sound of a chain coming from not far off in the woods.

Richard whistled softly for the men and he and Black drew their swords silently as the other men quickly gathered, conditioned to that warning silently gathered with their weapons in hand. Ever so slowly and quietly they spread out a bit and fumbled their way through the wooded area around the field. Black was giving the signal every few steps to stop and listen. Something was out there he knew it and he was going to find it. He feared that a bandit or two made it to safety and were now on their way back to extract revenge. Black was determined to get the best on them. As they listened, all ears on high alert the sound came again. Black signaled to Cron his right hand man that when he gives the signal the two would rush the tree that was harboring the bandit, while the others bring up the rear and circle around.

Black gave the order he and Cron rushed the tree, running to the other side. Swords drawn and ready to strike anything that moved. But what they found was the most shocking site that Black has ever encountered. Laying against the tree was what Black thought at a glimpse was a woman. He called for a torch and the group slowly walked closer to the heap on the ground next to the tree. Black leaned in carefully and took in the situation as the others looked in horror at what they were seeing. A young woman chained to a tree, obviously it was some poor maiden the band had picked up along the way. The men where hushed as the pity ran its course. Assuming the worse the men figured they would bury this young woman and give her a proper grave unlike the bandits who did this.

Black too, was assuming the worse when he went in to examine the women. He found the chain end that hung on the back of the tree would move in the wind and make a slight clanking noise. Black passed the torch off to Cron a veteran of the horrors of this land. Cron was a man brought up in a loving home only to be orphaned at the age of ten by a band of men who tore through their village late one night. He raised himself and came to work for Blacks parents Lord and Lady Black. As with most of the men in this band they all have known Black for many years. They were loyal and would gladly give their lives for him if the occasion should arise. You could say they had a kin ship with each other, each with their own story to tell and most not a happy one but thanks to Black they had a future and friendship. However unlike the others Cron had a family of six kid's one born not too long ago, and he was anxious to finish the two day trip back home.

As Cron held the torch high Black kneeled down and took in the sight. A woman who for what he could see was maybe in her late teens. Her dark hair was disheveled and caked with mud or blood Black couldn't tell which in the torch light. He picked up her limp hand to take the chain cuff off of her wrist. He had seen

these before, they are made by local
blacksmiths to temporary hold a prisoner
until someone could come and get them.
But these were old and well used, Black
cursed under his breath for it made him
mad to think of this being used for this
purpose.

Shocked he was that the small hand
that he was holding was still warm. He
unclipped the cuff then the other.   The
woman's arms just fell limply to the ground
beside her. Black then leaned in and gently
as he could picked up the small woman,
took her in his arms to move her away from
the tree hoping that maybe he would still
find life within. The men and Black jumped
back as she moved her arm in a wave as if

to wave the intruders off or in a feeble attempt to fight Black off. Black now astounded that this creature was still alive, he grabbed her up in his arms and quickly with the other men in step went back to the temporary camp.

Cron and Richard approached him as they walked back, "Do you think she will make it, she looks like she is knocking on deaths door as we speak." Black didn't reply his jaw set solid and his face like a hard stone. He just wanted to get her back to the light of the fire so he could maybe salvage something these bandits had tried to destroyed.

In the fire light he laid her out and with the men gathered, he slowly but yet with urgency felt her arms and legs for broken bones, he looked for cuts on the exposed parts of her body. She lay there in a deep sleep, dressed in a moth eaten ripped up and filthy smock that they assumed was maybe white at one time. However upon looking closer, it was a tunic top that she wore and a man's at that. Black lifted the woman's head as Tripper handed him a cup of water. At first the women didn't respond but then she surprisingly accepted the water and drank greedily but very drunkenly. She then collapsed with her thirst sated a bit. Tristan brought his blanket and they wrapped her up in it and laid her out so that she might rest comfortably. She was in a deep sleep and Black decided it was best to let her sleep and see if she makes it threw the night.

The men settled in to their bedding areas, that were kept close together, it was silent for a while. Each taking in the situation and analyzing it. Tristan was the first to talk, "what are we going to do with her if she makes it through the night", he asked. Black didn't say anything he didn't answer; he didn't know what to do or where to take her. Cron spoke up next, "we could take her to the abbey, and they would know what to do with her." You fool she has obviously been used by them and they won't take a spoiled women in even if it wasn't her fault," Tristan said. What about you Cron do you think your woman would take her in, I mean what's one more child right?" Richard suggested with a playful grin. Then they all looked at Black who was looking deep into the fire; he wasn't listening to the conversation he was trying to figure out his options for the women.

Black was a tall man, standing about six feet two. His deep blue eyes are set off by his shoulder length black tendrils, that wisp around his face. He was a hard looking man for the ripe ol' age of thirty. His muscular build and strength came from years in the Queens service. He is a solitary man, and a man of very few words. These men with him respect him and follow him, but they also know to respect his privacy. He is a good leader and a quick thinker. His aunt made sure he was well schooled in weaponry as well as numbers and letters. This makes for a very dangerous combination in a man of his power. But right now he is dumb struck as to what to do next with this woman. He isn't a man who would have any idea what to do with a woman or how to even care for one. Black was like most single Lords he visited the pub every once in a while so his personal needs could be met. But this was a different situation, he wasn't interested in sleeping with this woman, in fact he wanted to protect her. Blacks jaw set in a steel grip as his thought took this turn. He wondered to himself were the hell that thought came from. He shook it off as he thought about what to do with the girl if she lives the night.

"We will just have to take her back with us and figure it out as we go, if she lives I'm sure we will find a place for her or we could find her family if they will take her back".
 Black said concerningly but yet with pity in his voice. Richards's brow crinkled at the thought of someone missing their daughter like this. He thought about his own sister and the pain he and his parents went through when she died just before her third birthday. She was a beautiful toddler healthy one day and deathly sick the next. The doctor tried everything he could to save her, but in the end her little life slowly drained and she left this world as so many children do in these hard times.

However Black was a stern man he took care of business and never emotionally got involved. It would take away from his work and his work was the most important thing to him, well with the exception for Mary his sister. They all turned in for what was left of the night while Black stayed up to take watch. His thoughts running wild and anger, that took hold of him as it did most of the time when he would dwell on the deeds of men like the ones they dispatched this evening. And to take an innocent girl and ruin her for their own pleasure was just the lowest and most unconceivable thing to him. He is a man of honor, propriety, and loyal.

Morning came as Black stood at the ponds edge watching the sunrise. He had checked on the girl periodically during the night to see if she had passed. He was startled out of his thought by a little ball crawling towards the woods. Black just stood and watched in awe for a moment, not knowing if he should laugh or pity the poor girl who was actually trying to get away. "Was she actually trying to get away, where did the little fool think she was going to go?" Then it hit him she may still think that they are the men who took her in the first place. Black being over six feet tall went in pursuit of her. He didn't have to hurry she was more cleaning the grass with her man's tunic then actually getting anywhere. The other men rose to the spectacle of the woman who was obviously trying to make a run for it but couldn't quite do it fast enough. Especially, since she didn't even have the strength to get on her feet. And, the site of Black walking up to her crawling body, with controlled effort, so he wouldn't scare the crap out of her, was a sight to behold. He trailed behind her for a few yards trying to decide what, was the best course of action for this situation.

The men smiled as they realized Blacks problem, he didn't know quite how to approach this situation. He had an awkward funny look about him. He looked over at the men and chastised them because he knew what they were thinking by their silly grins. Soon they all stood around the girl who seemed totally oblivious to the world around her. Dehydrated, dirty, hungry and hurting all over, the girl stopped suddenly, aware that she was being watched. Her heart sank as her body gave out, no strength to pull herself away from these men.

She slowly turned to lay on her back and looked at the group standing around her. Fear choked her very life, she was caught and now they would finally kill her. She gathered every ounce of strength she had and even some strength by shear will she tried to stand. She was going to face them head on; she wanted to memorize each face as the last bit of life left her body. The men just stood dumb founded by what they were seeing. And as she achieved height she looked from one face to another staring down her foe head on. But then it hit her, these were not the men who took her in the first place. So what did they want with her.

Just then Richard ran off to the pond and returned with a cup of water. The other men looked at him with a kind of smirk. He held out the cup from a distance just far enough for her to reach it with little effort. She stared at him and started to back away when she lost her footing, which wasn't very good today anyways. But as she fell backwards strong arms wrapped around her waist and stopped her from the inevitable fall to the ground. She instantly looked up over her shoulder to see a man with dark brown wavy hair. Black swung her up into his arms and carried her back to the fire. A couple of men began to restoke the fire. Dirk one of the men also elected early on to be the cook of the group whipped up a quick meal from left over dried beef and beans.

The girl sat silently taking it all in. She sat off away from them, that's where the big man deposited her and that's where she decided to stay. She caught glimpses being thrown her way as a man or two stole a look at her. Black on the other hand stood away from her as he assessed her. Her hair was dark but how dark he couldn't tell it was matted with dirt or maybe blood and dirt. Her skin was covered in mud; there is no telling how long this girl has been stuck to that tree. Her arms and legs, what little he could see were scratched up and he could see dried spots of blood. After a bit he approached her, but the look on her face told him that she was very skittish and who would blame her. He kneeled down in front of her, "What is your name" no answer she just looked at him, "can you tell me your name"? She looked at him without answering him. She stared at him but he noticed it wasn't a blank stare like you would get from one who was possessed or have mental problems. She seemed to be assessing him and that unnerved Black a bit. "Maybe they cut her tongue out", Cameron chimed in. Everyone looked over at Cameron who was standing among the crowed giving him a look of surprise, "WHAT, everyone knows woman's mouth can drive a man insane with their talking". Cameron just shrugged as if to say, you know you all were thinking it to.

Black rose to his feet looking down at the girl, "well we'll take her to Mary maybe she can do something with her". With that the men broke off and started to break camp. Within no time they were on their way. Richard went over to the girl and offered his hand; she just looked at him and seemed to be decided what he wanted. "If you would like I can help you up and you can sit with Black, we have no extra horses and I don't think you will make it far on your feet.

She decided she had no choice but to comply with the man. She got up without taking his hand and followed as he led her to Black who was already up on his massive horse. She looked at the horse, and the horse seemed to acknowledge her and dipped his head. Her gaze then turned to the man they called Black, but before she could think Richard grabbed her under her arms and lifted her up so that Black could position her on the horse. This is going to be a long day thought Black as he set the girl in front of him, she didn't weight but maybe a few stones but she smelled like she had been laying in a barn for a month without bathing.

They road most of the day, Black would glance down at the girl to find her staring back up at him. At some point midday she fell asleep with her head on his chest. That evening they made camp and Dirk set to work getting some kind of meal started. Black wanted get as far down the road as he could so he opted to eat on the road with Dirk handing out dried beef sticks. The girl ate hers and Black could tell that she was hungry so he offered her his as well. She took it and had it was gone before the others had time to finish theirs. Now at least she will get a meal and some drink, maybe she will talk now, he thought to himself still trying to figure out what to do with her.

As Black slide from the horse and turned to help the girl down he made a decision to give her a chance to bathe. He went to his bags draped over the back of the horse and pulled out a sliver of soap. He handed it to the girl and called Richard over. "Do you have a pair of pants and shirt she can use till we can get her to Mary"? Richard ran off to his horse and grabbed what was requested and returned with the clothing in hand. Richard handed them to the girl and Black pointed at a stream not far out of view. When she looked questioningly up at him, he took a deep breath and trying to retain his patience he pointed again and instructed her to go to the stream and wash up, and told her that when she was done there would be food.

The girl walked off slowly towards the stream glancing at the men who were taking in the conversation to some delight. She did stink she could smell it and she decide it would do good to clean up so she could see what damage had been done. When she got to the stream she glanced back to notice that no one what watching her, the thought of running entered her mind, but left just as quickly, she didn't know where she was and had nowhere to go. Taking off her stained and smelly tunic she walked into the water that was maybe two feet deep in its deepest part. A stream she could handle, it was large bodies or deep water, "black water" she called it that she was afraid of. First she washed her hair, soaping it and rinsing it several times. She then soaped up her body and rinsed, she examined herself to make sure she was clean, then left the water and donned her new clothing. She returned to camp and sat off a ways from everyone as she picked at her hair, sort of brushing it as well as she could.

Black was in deep thought trying to think of what to say or ask. What was most important to know from her? "Do you have a name"? She looked at him and slowly without taking her eyes off her him nodded a yes. "Good, well what is your name"? She just looked at him with what he sensed was pleading, but for what he couldn't figure out. Then he asked "do you have family, what's your family's name"? She continued to just stare at him. Then appeared what looked like a tear in the corner of her eye. Then Black decided to just ask, "Can you talk"? She slowly nodded her head NO. "But you can understand what I'm saying"? She nodded yes. "Did they cut your tongue out"? Oh for all that is holy why in world did I just ask her that, he was going to kill Cameron for even suggestion that. But the girl just slowly answered NO with a slow nod of the head.

Just then Richard approached with a plate of food for each of them. He sat next to Black and gave him a questioning look. Black just heaved a sigh and shook his head; this was going to be difficult if she couldn't communicate with them. When Black and Richard looked back to the girl she was wolfing down her portions of food. She could feel her strength retuning with every bite.

Chapter 2

The big house loomed in the distance. Black was relieved to see home. The men too were glad to be back and couldn't wait to take some much needed rest. Richard, Tristan, Cameron, Justice and Dirk all resided with Black at his manor. Tristan took care of the animals, the horses, hunting dogs. He was a tall slender man, but had battle scars to show his power and experience. His weapon of choose was the battle ax and even though he was tall and slim he had strength. Cameron was in his mid-thirties he was a man of few words, and when he did talk it was usually something that would offend most. He slept in the barn with Tristan and helped out were ever he was needed.   His build was almost six feet and he had muscles that almost made him look shorter than his six foot stature. His weapon of choice was his sword, and he was good at wielding it. Justice or The Judge as they sometimes called him; he liked to think of himself as judge and jury when hunting criminals. But he also had an aristocratic side to him. Unlike the other two he preferred a bed to sleep in and he like to be clean all the time. But he was a man with a purpose and that was to stamp out evil in his country. His weapons of choice, what daggers, and a sword. He was quick and could kill a man with his bare hands if he had to. Dirk was the oldest of the group in his late thirties he was already showing gray hairs. He was built and like the others was a man with a mission. Dirk towered at just over six feet tall he was the voice of reason and a good cook. His weapon of choice was also the sword. He like the others came from families with money, they all studied there use of weapons as an apprentice from a knight. Cron was the one who was different he had a wife and six children one that is just weeks old and he was anxious to get home to see them. From a young age he learned to covet what was his. His family was killed by bandits but he was raised up under the watchful of the Lord and Lady Black and after there deaths Blacks Aunt. He was more a brother to Black and Mary. He had a home a few miles away and he longed to be there now. All these men earned their Knight Hood from the queen, they have fought in wars together and they have kept the piece in the queen's name. Now they are her secret police, they roam the country side and search out the despicable of the land to bring them to justice.

But Black, as hard as he was he was dreading what he hoped wouldn't be too much of a confrontation with his sister Lady Mary. As they rounded the drive in front of the manor he could see her stepping out of the house through the large doors. She always came to greet him when he came home, now he just hoped she wouldn't make a big deal of it when she see he brought home a girl something he has never done before. But what choice did he have he couldn't leave her there and he didn't know where to take her. He didn't even know her name.

Mary however upon seeing the frightful sight of a women wrapped in a blanket in the arms of her brother was anything but upset. Amused at the sight before her, her brother doesn't take women and to see him protectively holding one now was something she wished she could preserve for a life time of humor. She ran out to them, Richard dismounted and helped the girl to her feet. She was conscious of the women now standing a few feet from her and she recoiled and backed right into a hard muscular chest. She spun around and used Black's body to hide herself from the women. Black looked at Mary who was smiling, "her I knew it smile at Black". "We found the bandits and then we found her, I didn't know what to do with her she won't talk or can't talk, we don't even know her name I thought you might know what to do with her." Mary looked at her brother even though it wasn't what she thought, she knew better then to think otherwise, this girl needed her help and she would do what she could.

Black turned to the girl and softly said, "This is Mary she is going to help you and get you some proper clothing, she is safe and will take good care of you." The delight in Mary's eyes was growing, it will be like having a sister, she thought to herself. But the state of the women and the trials of what she has gone through at the hands of others made her heart fill with pity and sadness for her. Mary tried to take a step forward but the girl just buried herself into Black's chest trying to escape some unknown fate. Black gently took the girls shoulders in his hands and over his shoulder told Mary to hold out her hands so that she could see that she meant no harm. The men stood and held their breaths as they watched Lord Black's act of gentleness a sight they have never seen.

Mary held out her hands for the girl to see and maintained a smile, although her hopes were being dashed at the thought that this girl was maybe mentally off somehow. However, the girl peeked around the big man and sheepishly looked at Mary's hands and then to her face to find confirmation that she was in fact safe. Mary then held out her hand for the girl to take but it took a few more seconds for the girl to study the situation. She looked up into Black's eyes like a child who was lost, and found strength there as he told her it was okay for her to go with Mary.

She then slowly reached out and Mary took her hand gently and led her into the house. Black gave his orders as the men dispatched to their duties. They were gawking at the man, there leader the hard as stone complexity of this man was just melted by a girl. They couldn't wait to see how this unfolded right before their eyes.

Mary led the girl through the parlor, up the stairs to the hallway with rows of rooms. "We are going to have to get you cleaned up, and get you some clothes. I think you will fit nicely into mine we seem to be the same size." Mary chattered up a storm trying to ease both their minds. The girl just followed her without a word, letting Mary take her where she will. The hallway was long and lined with several sets of double doors. There were pictures of people hanging on the wall as they walked the corridor. There were pictures of men in their dressy clothes and family pictures some looked ancient and some looked to be only a few years old. The hallway was very wide and every door was closed, it was lined with some chairs and small long tables with flowers and some had small paintings of flowers. The light was dim but night was falling and the girl could see the red orange of sunset through the windows at the end of the hall.

"This is my room", Mary said cheerfully as they entered the last doors in the hall way. "We'll find you something to wear and then I will get the maid to bring water so you could bath. I have some really pretty smelling soap that smells like roses I think you will like that." Mary kept up the chatter to keep the air around her from going silent; she went to her wardrobe and picked out a green light fabric dress with some soft toed slippers for the girl to wear. Mary pulled a cord by her door and within seconds a young girl entered the room. She was given orders to have the tub brought to her room along with warm water. The girl curtsied and nodded her understanding and hurried off. Mary then turned to the girl and to her surprise she was hiding around the side of the wardrobe. Mary thought to herself that she didn't take the serving girl as a threat to her into consideration. "It's okay, I'm sorry I didn't think before I acted, I hope you could forgive me. That was Sarah she is my maid and is as nice as the day is long. You can trust her she won't hurt you, nothing and nobody will hurt you hear. Not as long as you are under Adrian's care."

Mary could see the girl was confused, then it came to her, I mean Black he is my brother, Black is our family name his real name is Adrian." The girl showed signs of understanding and to Mary that was a good sign that maybe she did have some mental worth.

A short time later though the girl was back in the corner hiding beside the wardrobe again as the helpers brought the large basin and water in as Mary had asked. She let her hide in there till everyone was gone, then coaxed her out and asked her if she knew what a tub was for. The girl nodded yes and so Mary handed her the soap and laid out a towel and the dress for her. "I'm going to leave you to bath are you going to be okay by yourself or do you wish me to stay." The girl just looked at her and Mary took it that she knew what to do. "Good I will be back shortly for you, I will see that you are not disturbed." The girl nodded to Mary as she left the room. Now Mary was going to find her brother and find out what was going on and who this girl was.

Mary found her brother just as he was leaving the stables. Now he knew she was going to hit him with a ton of questions that he couldn't answer. "There you are I think you have a little talking to do my *lord*. Who is this girl and how did you come about having her in your care." Black rolled his eyes he knew he had to find answers out but he didn't really have much to tell Mary. "We found the Troupe Gang bedding down

a few nights ago in a small field. We rallied
and attacked when it was done none were
standing. During the night Richard and I
heard a noise in the woods so I rallied the
men thinking it was one of the bandits." He
stopped not knowing how much he should
tell. His sister was a gentile women and the
condition of the girl when they found her is
hard for him to stomach, how would she
take it. "You can tell me Addie I am a grown
women now." Black contemplated it then
thought he might as well tell her the truth.
 "She was chained to a tree and had been
for a few days at least, I didn't know what
to do with her I thought you might. So here
we are and there she is." Mary was
flabbergasted the thought that someone
could be treated so callously, now she

understood why she was so shy and skittish. However the truth be known they were all on a journey of discovery that will both horrify them and give them much to be thankful for.

Chapter 3

Mary returned to the house and went
up the stairs to her room and knock softly.
When there was no answer she slowly
opened the door and whispered that it was
only her and that she was coming in. To
Mary's shock the girl was standing naked in
the middle of the room. The girl looked at

home, being naked as the day she was born. This was odd to Mary being very conservative. The girl looked at Mary as if she was all of a sudden ready to run. Mary went to the tub and grabbed the large towel she left for her. Walking slowly she approached the girl with a smile and the towel and covered the girl.

Mary felt a tinge of pain as she could see scars and bruises on her body. Because she had been standing naked Mary could see scars that she thought looked like whatever the cause was it must have been painful.

The sun was setting so Mary lit a few candles and the oil lamps on the wall to get some light into the room. She smiled at the girl, "would you like me to brush your hair. Come sit over here and I will brush it out for you." She led her to the chair and got her horse hair brush and gently started to brush the girl's hair.

Her hair was as dark as pitch and hung down her back. Mary noticed her beautiful light green eyes like the color of new grass and long dark eyelashes. She was about five and a half feet tall, slim with pale skin. This girl was beautiful and even Mary appreciated her beauty. Mary herself was a beautiful woman of eighteen. She wasn't married yet to her Aunts dismay. She was about five three with brown hair and blue eyes, slim and beautiful olive colored skin.

As she brushed the girl's hair she started to ask her questions. "Do you have a name that we can call you"? The girl just looked down, it was very hard to not be able to communicate but then again she was used to it by now. "Well how about I give you a name, would that be okay." The girl nodded, looking up at Mary and waiting expectantly for a name. "How about Elizabeth, no, Josephine, no you don't look like a Josephine." After a few more tries Mary came up with the name Catharine. "How about that name it's a beautiful name for a beautiful girl, do you approve." The girl nodded her head in approval. "Then it's done we will call you Catharine."

Mary finished bruising out Catharine's hair and helped Catharine to dress, then together they went down to the kitchen to find something to eat. The house was quiet and Mary wondered where her brother had gone to. She wanted to tell him the news about the new name.

As they sat and ate some cold left over's from lunch Mary decided to find out some more about this women. "Do you have a family?" Catharine just looked at her, not a blank stare but Mary could tell she didn't know how to answer her. "Okay yes or no questions, did you come from a family at some time?" Catharine nodded a solemn yes. She could tell it was something that made her upset. Mary knew she wasn't going to get anywhere tonight so when the girls finished they headed up the back stairs to the second floor.

Black was just coming out of the office that was the first room. "Ah there you are I wanted to let you know that we have found a name we are going to call her Catharine, fitting don't you think." Black wasn't paying much attention to Mary; he was aw struck by the beauty before him. Never had he seen such beauty in a women and now, can see the women and not the girl. "I'm sorry sis what did you say." It didn't escape Mary that her brother was taken by the beauty; Catharine on the other hand seemed to relax a little more with him around. "I am taking Catharine to her room; I thought the Green room would be a good match." Black nodded his approval as he shook off the need to stare at her. "Wait did you say Catharine, is that her name?" "No silly I already said I gave her a name and she approved." Fitting he thought as they walked off. He stood there transfixed and completely taken back by what he just saw.

Mary took her to the third door on the left down the hall and opened the door. The room was very large, with a dressing table a wardrobe and very large bed with a wooden canopy. It also had a sitting area with a couple chairs and a small table. A desk sat against the wall next to the double doors. The room was graced with two large windows draped with heavy grass green curtains. Catharine looked around the room she was uncomfortable and didn't understand what it was she was supposed to do there.

"This is your room; you are going to stay with us till we find out where you belong." That last statement sent chills up Catharine's spine. She never wanted to go back not there. "Well you must be tired so I will leave you to sleep; I had one of my night gowns laid out on the bed for you. You know where to find my room and Addie's room is right across from yours. Mary began to exit the room as Catharine followed Mary to the door. "See there that's Addie's room he is usually up all night anyways, so don't let his light bother you." Good night Catharine I will see in the morning for breakfast. Mary motioned to Catherine to go to the bed and as she stepped away Mary closed the door, wondering to herself if maybe she should stay with her on her first night. Instead she went to her room she had something else that she needed to do.

Catherin stood on the inside of the door, turning slowly to take in the room. She was scared of the dark so she left the light on. She walked slowly to the bed and began to undress as she kept watch on her surrounding, as if some unseen force would jump out and grab her. As she donned her night shift she stood in her newly acquired room and looked around, but still not making a move. She could hear the wind outside on the window. It sounded as if someone was tapping. This scared her beyond what she mentally could handle at the moment as memories flooded her mind. Catherine now with a tear streaked face and scared climbed on the bed to the head board and huddled there.

Hours later Black walked down the hallway and noticed that Catharine's light was still on. It was well into the night and he had been in his office preparing dispatches to the queen. Against his better judgment he went to the door and listened for a moment. He couldn't hear anything and figured she must have fallen asleep with the light on. Black quietly opened the door to extinguish the oil lamp. But instead he saw that Catharine was not only not asleep but huddled on the bed at the head board with her knees drawn up. When she caught sight of him she jumped out of bed and ran to him. Catharine buried her tear streaked face in his chest. "What is it

Catharine? " He walked her back to the bed and pulled down the covers and motioned for her to crawl in. "People are supposed to sleep in the bed under the covers." Black said with a small encouraging smile. Then it was out before he could think it through, "would you like me to stay a while till you fall asleep". Catharine nodded yes, so Black pulled a chair up next to the bed tucked her in and blew out the light.

Black sat in the moon lit room for what seemed like a lot longer then he should have. Catharine was, fitfully tossing and turning in her slumber. He watched the moon light reflect off her face as she slept. His mind was working, working on a plan to find out where or who she belonged to. He made a promise to himself one he doesn't make lightly. He would find her family and see to it that she is never hurt again. Black stood angry at himself, trying to figure out where that train of thought came from.

 This women was his ward, temporary ward and he will find out where she belonged and then deliver her safe and sound. Happy with that reasoning he quietly slipped out of the room and into his, where he spent the rest of the night deep in thought about what to do about Catharine next.

With morning came cooler weather now, winter wasn't far away. Black could smell the chill in the air and was content with the coming winter because he had finished what he set out to do before the onset of the dreaded cold months ahead. Black stood on the front steps to the manor, he noticed Mary and Catharine walking up, Mary with a smile on her face, Catharine on the other hand always had a scared little girl look, unsure, and frightened.

"Ah there you are Addie I was wondering, I have some things to take care of would you be so kind as to show Catharine around a little, just till lunch, maybe show her the chapel. Black nodded and Mary set out in some unknown destination towards the barn. "Well would you like to see our chapel Ms. Catharine?" She looked up at him and for a very brief moment he thought he caught a hint of a smile. Catharine nodded her approval and they started out through the house to the back. The house was very large it took a few minutes to reach the large double doors at the back side of the manor. The doors where very tall, almost oppressingly huge. Made out of dark stained wood, with a crosses etched in each of them.

"This is the family chapel. My parents were married here; my grandparents were also married here. My grandfather, father, my sister and I were all christened here." With that he opened the large doors. Catharine was taken aback by the high ceilings and colorful windows. She walked in slowly so as not to disturb anyone or anything. She walked down the aisle to a table in the front with Black slowly following behind. He watched her take it all in, keeping back giving her time to enjoy the beauty and comfort of the place. She stopped short of a alter table and stared intently at the cross that hung on the wall with the crucified Jesus. She reached for him but it was just out of reach. Turning to Black she pointed, giving him a look of questioning. He understood what she was asking, "it's Jesus, and he was crucified on the cross so that we could go to heaven. He died for our sins, that cut is when the guards stabbed him in the side to see if he was dead. They say water came out instead of blood. Have you ever heard the story of Jesus?" Catharine shook her head no; she was captured by the story and looked to Black to tell her more.

Black led her to a pew and they sat together while he told her stories of the bible he had learned as a child. He explained to her that they haven't had a service in many years, in fact since his parent's death. He was surprised the Catharine understood what he was telling her. He just couldn't figure out why she couldn't or wouldn't talk. Maybe she had an accident as a child, maybe she was just born that way. He didn't know and wondered if he ever would know.

Next Black took her to the library, "can you read Catharine" She nodded no and looked down like that was something to be ashamed of. In fact in this day and age it was rarer to find someone who could read. "You are welcome to use any of the books you like; maybe Mary and I could teach you some words." With that he got a big nodded yes. For a moment she looked happy and his suggestion of teaching her to read some seemed to make her happy.

Just then the door burst open and Richard ran in, causing Catharine to jump and panic until Black caught her in his arms. "You idiot you know you can't just burst in like that with her. " "I'm sorry My Lord but the mare is foaling, and I think it's going to be a rough one on her." Mary came in seconds behind Richard; by this time Catharine had recognized his voice and slowly came out from her hiding behind Black. They all went out together to the barn to see the new foal being born and to make sure it went the way it should. Catharine stood in amazement at what she was seeing. Black could tell she was experiencing this for the first time and she found joy in the new life. He was glad for this, to see her on pins and needles watching with wide eyes and all the pined up excitement of a little girl. The foal took a little while coming and Black was worried for a bit that the mare might have a problem birthing, but eventually the foal was born and both mother and baby where fine. With the sun setting and the crispness in the air Black thought it would be best if they headed back to the house and let the men watch over the new foal.

They sat and ate cold left over's in the kitchen, Mary and Black talking about things going on. They could sense Catharine watching the back and forth banter of the two. How they laughed, and they even caught her smiling a few times. When they finished Black walked the girls to the second floor, Mary kissed his cheek and bid him and Catharine good night as she walked off to her room. They watched her go and when her door closed Black opened Catharine's door and lit her oil lamp. Once again before he could think before talked he offered to stay until she went to sleep. She nodded yes and started to undress to put on the night cloths Mary had given her. Black was taken by surprise she didn't seem to care that he was in the room. He quickly averted his eyes, "I will wait outside until you are ready." He quickly exited the room trying to avoid what his body instantly told him he wanted. Unfortunately for him to his bad luck Justice came down the hallway. His room was at the end across from Mary.

As he sauntered by he gave Black a mischievous grin, and let out a manly cover up cough. "It's not what you think I am just checking up on her." As if it couldn't get any worse Catharine opened the door and stood in the door way in her night shirt. Justice bowed and crossed him arm, "and a very good night to My Lady Catharine." With a smile and a smug look he winked at Black and practically danced down the hallway in delight, he couldn't wait to tell the others. Catharine looked at Black she didn't understand what had just taken place but Black knew and he will hear of it again and again.

Chapter 4

He slipped into the room with her and tucked her into bed. It was becoming a ritual with him; he had this undying need to see to her safety. He would watch as she would toss and turn in her sleep. He figured she had many demons in her nightmares. What he would give to be able to see what she sees and know where she came from, where she had been. As she slept he slipped from the room and crossed the hall to his own. The void that was with him, the not knowing how to help her it ate at him daily now. As he undress for bed he kept thinking about her, her nightmares, her skittishness even though she was getting use to people around her she still became jumpy at sudden movements from people. She seemed to live in a privet world and for the first time Black wanted to be a part of that world.

Black had sent a letter for Dr. Ivan explaining the situation and asking him to come as soon as he could. Unfortunately the doctor was out of town and had been for weeks. He was a trusted man and Black thought he could help uncover the mystery behind the women.

Days went by without Black staying in Catharine's room. She had adjusted enough to stay alone. Even though he knew she still didn't want to be left alone, she seemed to make an effort to. It made him uneasy; he felt that he was abandoning her. But to the best of his knowledge she slept alright now by herself in her own room. Until one night, when everything changed for Lord Adrian Nicolas Black.

After putting Catherin to bed he crossed the hall to his room. He undress and slipped into bed. Where, as a nightly ritual he lay there thinking the night away. Sometime a few hours after getting into bed as he was dosing off he heard his door creek. He sat up and waited to see who was coming and why. If one of the men came and got him at night it usually meant something was wrong. Since he wasn't clothed he waited sitting up, but it wasn't one of the men it was Catherin. She silently slipped into the room and slowly, quietly closed the door behind her.

"Catherine what are you doing, you shouldn't be in here it's not proper." He could see her in the oil light shivering in her night dress. Her eyes were pleading to him to let her stay. She pointed at the floor he understood but how could he allow her to sleep on the floor. "What is it, are you scared of the dark?" She shook her head yes. In his hast he jumped out of bed

before he realized his folly and the state of
his undress? Her expression didn't change;
she seemed unbothered by his nakedness.
 Crossing the floor to him in the middle of
room where he stood in all his glory she
approached him. She looked at his chest his
scars she began to trace them ever so
slightly with her finger tips. The big cut he
got in a fight with some highway men on his
shoulder. , the one across his chest and
belly. She walked around him tracing and
intently concentrating as if trying to absorb
each blow herself. When she rounded back
to the front of him she laid her palm on his
chest and looked up at him. Then put her
other palm on her chest. Then to his
surprise she gracefully stepped out of her
night shift. What he saw before him was a

sight that raised inside of him an anger that he had never felt. But yet a connection between them that drew them together.

There on her chest, shoulder and belly, even her upper legs, scars and cuts as serious as his. She gently grabbed his hand and with his fingers traced the scar on her shoulder, a scar that bore across one breast, under her other breast another scar; he walked as she did and stood behind her to find more scars. Understanding a little more, it was making a little more sense, the nightmares the skittishness. When he rounded to stand in front of her she was looking down. He gently pulled her chin up so she faced him. And in her eyes he saw her shame, anguish and betrayal. She had tears gently rolling down her cheek. Black wanted nothing more than to hold her and take away whatever it was that haunted her. He shook himself back into the present and realized that Catherine was standing in his room, naked. He walked to the cupboard and pulled out some leggings and quickly tied them in place. He went to her standing in the middle of the room, her eyes pleading for him to let her stay. "We have to take you back to your room Catherine it isn't a good idea to be in a man's room in the middle of the night, especially with no clothing. He picked up the discarded garment off the floor and started to put it over her head. She stopped him put her and on his chest and tried one last time. Looking up into his Black eyes she pleaded with him, than he saw her mouth move as she tried to form the word she wanted to express. He waited; he waited to see if he would hear her first words. "pleeezzaah", she said, sounding like a child trying to talk for the first time, pleading to be wanted, protected. Black stood paralyzed his thought process stopped as he heard her voice for the first time. He needed to prove to her that he would protect her that she was safe with him. In a moment, without thinking he bent down and kissed her lips. He could taste the saltiness of her tears.

She rested her palms on his chest as she took in the security of being there in his presence. She found strength in him a chamber of safety that she never had. He led her to the bed and with experience laid her down as he continued to kiss her lips and neck. He stopped and looked into her eyes and saw a trust there he had unconsciously wanted from the first day he met her. "Have you ever laid with a man before "? she nodded in confirmation it seemed to give his mind permission to precede, to continue loving her. He took one breast in his mouth and suckled one brest then the other. He kiss her belly and back up her neck before he slowly, almost leisurely spread her knees and positioned himself for entry. He couldn't stop now if he wanted, she was so perfect scars and all. He wanted her and he would have her. He looked down at her, her pupils dilated with pleasure.   Her breast swelled and her lips engorged with want. Slowly, he gathered his strength to hold back the wave that threatened to end this too soon, restraining to hold on to what little he had left of his sanity, as he slowly penetrated her warm depths. She cried out as he felt the resistance of her virginity. He was shocked and filled with instant turmoil she said she had laid with a man before. But the tear in her eye and the woman's skin his manhood was now resting against told him otherwise, he would be her first. It was too late to stop now, backing out a little he pushed in with just the amount of force that he needed to make Catherine a women, the barrier gave way and a small cry escape her lips he pulled out and reentered her again feeling her body tighten with the pain. He leaned in to her ear as he slowly pushed again and again. "The pain will stop in a moment, I'm so sorry Catherine I would never have done this if I had known". Finally he could feel her relaxing and see her pupils dilated again with pleasure. He kissed her more deeply this time feeling their tongues mingle together, slowing to a more gentle rhythm. Her breath came quicker as did his he could feel her climaxing, bringing on his own, until she suddenly let out sigh of pleasure as wave after wave raced through her. Black too found his climax letting out a loud whimper of pleasure as he spilled his seed into her.

He collapsed on her, spent and in wonder. Never had a women brought him so much pleasure, never has a women made him feel so alive. He felt her arms wrapping round his shoulder as he turned his head that was buried in her neck and kissed her cheek. "I'm so sorry Catherine I didn't know; please will you ever forgive me." He buried his head again in shame into the curve of her soft neck trying to find comfort there. It was then he felt her gentle reassuring kiss. Black slid off of her and lay at her side holding her close taking in the very sent of her. She has looked to him for security and strength and now it was him clinging to her. Loving her and never wanting to let her go.

As morning came Catherin woke and slipped out of bed, but not before brushing the sleeping man with a kiss. Standing next to the bed she watched him as he slept, memorizing every line, every curve of his features. He was so peaceful laying there as the early morning rays penetrated the window and washed him in golden rays of light. Leaving and returning to her room, there was no sound, the manor was quiet as all slept away the cold early morning hours. But not Catherine she climbed into bed content, amazed at the wonder she had experienced and now she was a little more hopeful for the ever unknown future.

As winter came and the days passed, Catherine spent much of her time in the beloved chapel, sitting with Mary or Black while they told stories of the man on the cross. Sometimes the men having nothing to do would join in the story telling however, their stories of heroic actions differed from that of the man on the cross. The men loved the chance to tell a good tail and they could tell some whoppers about their many years together. Catherine filled with excitement as they weaved tails of Knights and the adventure stories of her beloved Black. Some nights they would sit in the parlor while Mary played soft lullabies on the harpsichord. Well until the men had enough of the soft lovely music. They would talk Mary into play some more upbeat music, to Black's horror it usually turned into pub music. But he watched as Catherine now laughing and clapping and some even got her to try her hand at dancing. Watching Dirk trying to dance with little Catherine was priceless and they all laughed there enjoyment. Mary too was enjoying having Catherine, enjoying the change in her. She had gotten used to the people around her in the manor and has almost lost that skittish, lost and frightened look she had.

She spent a lot of her time following one person or another around, not wanting to miss a single experience. She helped Richard in the Barn and Dirk cook. She was good with the animals spending time petting and making cooing voices to them even the dogs. She was there when the foal was born and she was there when the chicks hatched, she hovered close when Black's beloved hunting dog Millie gave birth to her eight puppies. And she cried for poor Millie and the puppy that didn't make it.

Most afternoons she sat in Black's office as he did his figuring or writing. She would pull books off the shelf and flip through the pages looking at pictures and pretending to read the words. It didn't matter what she did as long as she had her Black and constant human connection.

She hasn't spoken a word since that night, although she was starting to make noises, Black loved to listen to her laugh, or the baby crooning noises she made to the animals. Sometimes she would sit alone in the chapel and Black could hear at the door her soft babbling. She no doughtily was talking to the man on the cross in her own way. On one visit from Crouch Black took him back to the chapel to hear her talking and Crouch surprised as he was that she made a sound at all, he reassured Black that she seemed to just be going thru the same motions of a child learning to talk. It made Black happy to think that she was doing this because of him; even though she never did it if she knew someone was around. He loved her; he couldn't quite admit it yet to her out loud or anyone around him. Although they all knew, seeing him with her, his protectiveness over her and his watchful eye. He changed too; he was relaxed, happy and even laughed and joked with everyone. Gone it seemed the ridged man, gone the almost once heartless, hardhearted and unsympathetic man with only one mission in life. Now he had a new mission, Catherine and the very promise he made to her.

The nights however he no longer spent alone. In her room or in his it didn't matter as long as he had her in his arms. Some nights they made love till dawn others they he just held her while she slept. He would steal kisses in the hallways, in the barn, where ever he could get one. He wanted to be with her all the time, no matter what the task was. The funniest thing to watch one afternoon was when Mary decided to teach her how to embroider. She explained the finer points of the task and showed her what she could do. Catherine however didn't like this game at all. While Mary would be working away at her fabric, Black would see Catherine's attention else were. She even fell asleep next to Mary one afternoon and fell right into her lap, but woke quickly as Black belted out a laugh. Soon, to Catherine's delight the lessons stopped and she was once free again to roam.

One afternoon as the winter months were breaking into the warmer days of spring. A rider approached and Black immediately went to meet him. Even though it was warmer the sky was overcast and it had been raining off and on all day.

It was Doc Ivans, "hello my son", he said showing his happiness to see him and embracing him with a fatherly but manly hug. "Doc I'm so glad you're here I take it you got my message," "Yes and I became quite curious about your young Ms. Catherin." Black led him to the parlor where the men were sprawled out enjoying a lazy day of nothing. Doc took a seat as Black turned to Richard, "do you know where the girls went to," "I'll give you one guess," said Richard. "Could you retrieve them and have them come to the parlor for me, Mary will be excited that Doc was here and I want Catherine to meet him." Richard gave a nod and strode off to get the girls. "So do you have any new ideas about this girl, any new developments since your letter?" "No but you have to meet her, this whole situation would be much easier if she would talk. I know she can I have heard her." With that the girls entered Mary ran to Doc and embraced him, Catherine however started her retreat from the new comer. Black anticipating it stepped in behind her so all she would get for her efforts was a large wall of muscle. He gently put his hands on her shoulders, "this is Doc he has been a part of our family for many years, and he is a good man, smart and gentle." Catherine more trusting of his words slowly let Black lead her in to meet the good Doctor. Black sat her down in a chair opposite of the Doctor as Black took the seat next to her. "You didn't over exaggerate she is skittish around ones she doesn't know." You don't even know the half of it he thought to himself.

After a bit of talking to ease the tension in the atmosphere with Catherine. The Doctor started to raise out of his chair, "Well my good men I am tired and would like to wash for dinner, if you will excuse me I will show myself to my room." With that he leaned over the chair and pulled his black doctors bag out and turned to leave. What happened next shocked them all.

Catherine is known for her deep scrutinization of situations and people. She had been studying the good Doctor the way he talked, mannerism, even the very wink she caught him giving her in a fatherly way. Catherine had virtually decided that Doc was a good man. His eyes seemed wise and kind. His words easy to follow and pleasant to listen to, he had a soft wrinkly face that Catherine liked to look at because when he talked his chin and lower cheeks jiggled. But what she wasn't prepared for what his next actions or her own.

Doc collect his bag and pull it out from beside his chair as he swung the bag around to take his leave, Catherine poll vaulted out of her chair with a instant look of fear that even Black with his ability to predict her movements didn't see coming. She was instantly breathing heavy, wild like a caged bear, as she threw herself with the force of a man over the back of the chair to get away from some unseen force. Black moved in to stop her but to his surprise she dodged him. She was in a wild frenzy looking quickly for a way out instantly calculating her path. Black caught a glimpse of something in her face that made him fill with a fear, it was one of her demons haunting her and something triggered it but he didn't know what. Before any of them knew it, she was running full force for the door then the front door. Instantly Black set into motion acting on shear fear for the one he loved and the many years of experience, he made the whistle he made to rally his man and instantly they all understood. The whole incident only took seconds and even with the shocked looks still on their face they took flight after the poor women running scared from a demon they couldn't see or even imagine. They were not only set into motion by Black the man they have followed for years but for the love each one of them have developed for the poor women child. And now they all had the deep felling of a need to protect and care for her.

They were in hot pursuit of her as she dashed out the front door, Black in the lead trying to catch her before she could hurt herself.   One little women running wild being chased by seven grown men and them being trailed by an old man and a young women. The rain started to fall and there was a little chill in the air as Catherine hit the porch and down the front steps where she almost lost her footing only to quickly recover and take off across the large expanse of the grasses yard. She didn't have a plan nor was she thinking she was just getting away. Black was nearly caught up to her when she slipped on the wet muddy grass. But she jumped up and bolted again. Black finally caught her he was coming up behind when all of a sudden she hit the ground, and hard. She was instantly covered from breast to toes in mud. She jumped up holding her gut tight and slightly crouching. The men caught up and they instinctively formed a circle around the wild women. She looked around wildly for a way out of the barricade of men. They didn't mean anything to her, at that moment she just needed to survive. As the circle of men enclosed in on her she leaned in unexpectedly and grabbed a dagger out of Justices belt, Wielding it wildly in a stay back warning. Black tried frantically to connect with her to bring back to the present. He yelled her name but she didn't hear or respond to any of them. Black was beside himself filled with an emanating fear of the unknown. He didn't know what to do or how to bring her back to him. Suddenly while clutching the dagger loosely in her hand she grabbed again at her stomach. Black and the others could see something was very wrong. She was in pain although by the stance she had and the look on her face you wouldn't know it.

She brushed at her abdomen while protecting herself from the men, trying desperately to shake off the rising pain and feeling of vomit etching into her throat. The ground seemed to be pulling her in, trying to drag her down into darkness. She stood her ground but Black and the men knew what ever was wrong was getting worse by the minute. Black finally reached out for the dagger and she swiped at him.

But it worked he had her attention. "Please Catherine put the knife down before somebody gets hurt". She looked at him with a wild blank stare, he didn't know if he was even getting through to her. Her pupils he could see were so large they made her beautiful green eyes almost blackened by them, like a cornered cat. Black pleaded with her, letting her know that no one was going to hurt her and that everything was as it should be. He's not sure if any of it registered in her mind but she dropped the knife, Justice immediately retrieve it as Black went in. But a split second later she fell to the ground clutching her abdomen. Without hesitation Black scooped her up into his arms and immediately started back to the house with everyone in tow. "Put her in her bed Addie, quickly." Mary ordered, with concern written on everyone's face she took control of the situation. Catherin was soaked from head to toe and her skin was very cold to the touch. Doc arrived and started to give orders as the men stood motionless in the hallway, waiting for some kind of news. Black deposited Catherin on the bed, Mary could see the concern stamped on his face and body movements. They all knew he loved this women but to what extent none new. "Get her clothes off before she catches her death," Doc ordered. Mary pulled the wet clothes from her as Doc shut the door to hide the woman's nakedness from the men in the hall. Black picked up the still unconscious and now naked women from the bed as Mary striped the bed of the muddy wet coverlet. Doc then pulled the remaining covers back as Black redeposit her in the bed. But as Mary hastily pulled the cover up Doc stopped her. "Wait what in God's name." he said as he leaned in to take in the brutal scaring on her body. Mary too leaned in and with a look of horror on her face covered her mouth to silence a gasp. Mary had a glimpse the first night of Catherin's scars but not like this. On the other hand Black averted his eyes trying to not give any hint that he already had seen this, on *many* occasions. Mary pulled the covers up to Catherin's chin; she couldn't bear the sight of it any longer. Doc stared into the eyes of the man he has known all his life, without taking his eyes off

him he told Mary, "Mary would you be so
kind as to get us some tea and a pitcher of
water." Mary looked up and saw the two
men locked, so she wiped the tears from
her eyes and regained her composer and
headed to the kitchen.

Chapter 5

As soon as the door shut Doc took his eyes off Black to turn and slowly sit in the sitting chair. "Would you ask one of your barbarians to retrieve my bag so I can see if we can't help this poor child?" Black went to the door and quietly asked Richard to retrieve the doctors bag, he left to do his bidding. "you all might as well make your selves comfortable I'm afraid this is going to be a long night." Richard returned with the bag and found a set along with the others in the hallway. Black closed the door picked up a chair and sat at the beside of Catherine. Doc already knew what the cause of her pain was but until he could confirm any of his suspicions he wanted to verify it. He like everyone else wanted answers. But Doc had a feeling he knew what those answers would be and he knew that it wasn't going to be easy on the man that he knew without a doubt loved this women above all others. But if what the Doc suspected was true, he know Black would loose everything he has become to right this wrong.

Mary returned with the tea and water. Doc took out his bag and instantly it made sense to Black the bag! "When you took out your bag, that's it, that's when she bolted, it's the bag." To Blacks surprise Doc just shook his head. He suspected as much. As Mary poured them tea Doc began to tell what he suspected. "First you should know I have seen these scars before. On her hip is an X scar there is meaning behind that scar, a mark or a brand of some kind." "What exactly do you mean a brand, you mean like cattle brand." "Unfortunately yes, I have seen this brand on several bodies over the years, young men and women, their bodies mutilated and dumped in fields, and the sides of roads. Several of my trusted colleges and I have been trying for years to locate and dismember a secret society that has been a plague on the country and a thorn in the Queens side. Talk of grotesque experiments by so called doctors, sexual orgies, indulging in lude and disgusting acts of sex.   Usually boys and young girls fall victim to them.   Rumor has it that they use these poor children, in disgusting sex rituals or to for fill sexual fantasies.   It's a closed society and those who go there would die before they reveal the location or names of those involved. They dispose of the dead bodies regularly, some I have seen violated in the crudest manner possible."   Black looked at the women lying unconscious in the bed, he was sinking into a deep despair for the women he loved for what she must have gone through but anger was rising with each passing minute. His brain was already working out a way to exact justice.

"My guess is that your bandits robbed whoever is behind this secret society and while doing so they found your Catherine and took her as a spoil, probably to use at their personal use. The fact that she is even alive now is astonishing. It's said that children who are taken as slaves into this society are lucky to live past ten or twelve. But your miss Catherin I am assuming is close to eighteen years. There for I am going to assume that she was used for experimenting, she must be one hell of a survivor. Tell me Black was she a virgin when she came here?" Black looked down as he answered in a low deep, "yes". Mary shot him a look and then smiled knowingly at her brother, as Black averted his eyes. A very un-doctorly "humph" came from him. "thought so" he said. "Well we might as well head to the parlor, nothing we can do here until she wakes and that could be minutes or hours."

Black, Doc and the other men except Richard headed to the downstairs to the parlor. Black wanted to get more information on this secret society. As soon as everyone disappeared down the stairs Richard slipped in and saw Mary sitting next to bed. "Is she going to be all right Mary"? "I don't know, I don't know how one could overcome the life she has lived, and there's no telling how long she lived like she did." Richard held out his arms and Mary gladly went to him. He leaned down as he crushed his lips to hers. "Addie had been in such a good mood I was going to tell him about us, but now …. I can feel his heart breaking for her." "All our hearts are breaking for her Mary, but it's been a year and a half." Richard said with pleading eyes. "I know as soon as the time is right I will tell him." With that Richard slipped from the room and headed down to meet up with the other men before any suspicion arose of him and Mary.

They had been secretly courting for a long time now He wanted to marry her. But Black was always on a mission, of one kind or another. And he was a formidable presence to deal with at times. But since Catherin came into his life he was different, everyone sees it, and Mary and he should have told him while the going was good. Then maybe they could court out in the open and not have to hide their love by stealing kisses in a dark hallway.

Richard entered the parlor, the men sitting in a tight circle discussing information about this secret society and poor Catherin. Black and Doc told them what they found but kept some things personal like the scaring that covered her body. Black thought it was something that shouldn't be share publicly. "My Lord, Mary wanted me to tell that she is waking up now." Black practically ran to her side. Everyone was still amazed at the power this women child had over him. Then again she had some kind of a power over everyone.

Doc stood up and slowly shook his head, "well boys I'm afraid that Lord Black and Lady Mary are in for a long night tonight. Stay close in case you are needed. After this afternoons run thru the park I won't leave anything to chance. This poor girl needs our help to find out who she is and to try and help her fight the demons that haunt her memories." They all shook their heads in agreement. "And boys I am afraid that your Lord Black may need your friendship the most before the night is through."

Doc entered the room slowly holding his hands out to show he wasn't going to harm her. She still had a very unsure look in her eyes. But Doc knows what set her off in the first place and that was what he was planning to tackle first, the bag. He slowly made his way to the chair and sat in a way that she could see that he wasn't pulling any tricks. Black was grateful that the Doc took so much care in proving to her that he meant her no harm.

"Now listen to me Catharine, I am here to help you do you understand." If she did she didn't acknowledge it, she just stared. "I know you understand every word I'm saying, the problem isn't that you have a problem comprehending you just can't talk and I am going to try to figure out why, do you understand this Catharine." She nodded slowly. "I am going to start off slowly simple questions and I want you to answer them with a yes or no not a nod, do you understand this." She looked at Black with eyes of uncertainty; she doubted her ability to answer.

"Do you have a name?" Catherin tried to form the words with her lips but what her brain was telling her to say her mouth didn't seem to understand. "Take your time, take it slow and answer yes or no." Her mouth moved slowly as she tried to make the sound that she was trying for. "eeehhhssss" She said and Doc nodded his approval with a smile. "Good, do you know what your name is?" This time it took a lot longer for her to try the words. She turned to Black to find strength and for approval that she was doing what he wished. "eehhss" and she nodded to affirm her answer, making sure that it was understood. "Good, you're doing a great job. Now can you say your name for us?"

Once again she looked at Black as she focused on saying a word that she kept in the back of her mind all these years. "Vikkkkrrryyy", she shook her head shaking it off to try again, "Viiiikkkkkrrrrryyy, vvviiikkkkkkktttttrrrryyy". Blacks eyes lit up, "are you saying your name is Victory?" She nodded profusely in confirmation. "So they called you Victory, now can you tell me who called you Victory?" She racked her brain trying to remember how to say the words she had the memory of the people before. They were faded and worn memories but Victory kept them locked away deep inside. "Mmmmaaaammaaawwww", she mouthed and said in all most a whisper.

"Paawwwppppawww". "Mama and Papa is that what you are saying". She nodded then corrected herself, "yyeeess, RRRRhhhiikkkyyyy". "Mama, Papa, and Ricky, is this what you are saying." Victory nodded her mouth hurt and she was getting a head ach.

Doc thought on this for a moment, he could tell she was tiring of trying to talk. "Listen to me Victory, what happen to your parents and this Ricky?" She quickly made a motion dragging her finger across her throat. "They are dead, how did they die". Doc was starting to see that she had the memories to tell her story the problem was telling it. She simply said, "Man." "Are you saying that man killed your parents?" "Yeesss." "Did you see Man Kill your

110

parents?" She shook her head no. Black became lost in thought, and trying to digest, so much information was coming through tonight; finally a picture was being drawn. He was beginning to think it might have been better to just leave things as they were.

"Okay Victory listen to me because this is very important. You know my black bag, the one that sent you running?" Victory looked down as she sat up in bed, ashamed that she had reacted that way, and all the trouble she caused. "I am going to put the black bag on the bed, it is closed and I am not going to touch anything inside of it. I will then sit in my chair over here and I want you to open the bag for me." Victory shook her head no vigorously she couldn't do it. Black sensing her fear rising stood to move beside her, but Doc stopped him and told him to sit down that this was between him and Victory. "The only way I can get her to move past this is to engage her actively to explore so she will trust me. I can't do her any good if she won't let me help her; I know this is hard for you Black but you will have to trust me. If you don't than she will never trust me. She follows your queue Black; she wants to have your approval for everything she is doing. This is fine but you must not interfere with what I am trying to do." Black nodded and sat back down; he didn't like watching her go through this but understood the importance of it.

"I am going to put the bag on the bed, don't worry it won't hurt you. It is very important that you do this; you have to face the fear of this bag. Did this Man have a bag like this?" She nodded. "You need to understand that this is not Man's bag this is mine. I know that he used the things in his to hurt you. I use the things in this bag to help people as I am going to help you. You are going to find things in this bag that are the same as Man's but I won't use them to hurt you. Do you understand me Victory?" She nodded still unsure of this whole situation.

Doc lifted the black medical bag and slowly walked to the bed. Victory didn't move but she seem somewhat more relaxed. As if now that she knew it wasn't going to hurt her she might just look in it. He lowered the bag onto the foot of the bed. And when she didn't move he slowly backed away and sat in his chair. "Now Victory I want you to go to the bag and open it. Inside this bag are tools that you should recognize. Pick out those things and lay them on the bed for me. Do you understand Victory?" She slowly nodded her attention already on the bag as she crawled out of the covers and moved towards the bag. Mary immediately grabbed a smock to put on Victory's naked body. But Doc quickly but silently stopped her. You see her nakedness is more comforting to her then clothing. I believe that this woman has probably not worn a scrap of clothing until her disappearance.

Mary was flabbergasted this wouldn't work was she going to just run naked around the manor, she thought to herself. "Don't worry Mary she isn't going to stay that way; I just want her to be as comfortable as possible right now." Black realized that, that first night she came to him she wasn't bothered by his nakedness, it made sense now to him how she could just take her clothes off and stand before naked and without a trace of shyness.

Victory made her way towards the bag slowly, looking at it as if getting ready for some evil to pop out and grab her. First she felt the sides of the bag, running her hand up and down the leather. She moved her hand to the strap and buckle, slowly feeling as she unbuckled the latch on top.

Sitting back feeling very disturbed by the bag sitting in front of her, she paused thinking it through before she just reached over and snapped the bag open, jumping back a bit in case something came out at her. Doc watched her, pleased with himself that she had the personal strength to face her fear.

Victory leaned in as she squinted her eyes as if not wanting to see what was inside but her curiosity was getting the better of her. Slowly reaching her hand in she leaned over to see what was in the bag. First she pulled out a long thin knife about six inches long and half an inch wide. It was covered by a leather sheath; Victory didn't need to open it to know what it was she laid it on the bed. Reaching in again, she pulled out tongs and set them on the bed. She continued this until the bag was almost empty except for the medicines that were held in a leather pouch. Black dropped his head so that Victory wouldn't see the pain on his face as he watched her pull tool after tool out. Tools that he knew were supposed to be used to help people but in this case were used to hurt the women he loved. The horrors she must have felt, alone and hurting all the time. It made him want to hold her so tight that she imprinted on his body. He wanted to take the memories from her and replace them with good ones, of love, family and happiness. He would never let her feel such pain again, that he promised.

Doc speaking in a hush tone, easy and carefully thought out so as to take this to the next step. "Victory can you show me how Man used these things to hurt you?" She nodded but paused before she picked up the first tool the scalpel, closing her eyes she started to relive the things that were done to her. They could see tears starting in her eyes as she remembered the agony that this tool caused.

"Now you lay still and don't move or this will kill you. You don't want to be dead like your parents and brother. If you don't stay still I will have to put those ropes on you again." Victory remembered Man telling her this every time he hurt her. She didn't understand why he had to do this, cutting, pulling, stretching, prodding,

sewing, and the worse of all the breaking. Tears ran down as she held her eyes shut and played the memories one after another in her head. Suddenly she dropped the knife and backed away from the array of tools on the bed. She forgot some things that Doc didn't have in his bag. Victory rose from the bed, they watched as she seemed to search the room with purpose. She knew the things she had to add to the pile and search the room over. Finally coming to the wardrobe she swung open the doors and pulled out a few of the sashes. Victory ran to the bed and deposited them in the pile and turned to continue her search for the last thing she wanted to add to the pile.

She came to a stop next to Doc, as he sat patiently in his chair watching as she grasp the table next to him. With a mighty thunk she flipped the table over and all watched in amazement as she ripped the pedestal off the table, kicking the table top away to free it from its single leg, then smacking it on the floor to free it from its bottom legs that kept it from falling over. With a triumphant whack she through the six inch thick pedestal leg on the bed and wiped her hands off as to pat herself on the back. Black and Mary didn't understand the gesture but appreciated what was happening. Victory has faced her fears and looked as though she was now spitting on it.

Then a little winded Victory went and stood in front of Doc, yes in all her nakedness. She held out her hand to him to come see her pile. As Doc rose and walked to the bed, Victory turned to Black and beckoned him and Mary to come see. As the four of them stood at the foot of the bed they looked down at the tools that had destroyed this woman's youth, causing her anguish and unbelievable pain. Now she was ready to move on. A knock came at the door it was Dirk he asked if everything was okay. Black had to smile when he realized what Victory's antics must have sounded like to the waiting men in the hallway. Black told him everything was fine.

Dock turned to Victory and asked her if she could show him what the pedestal was used for. She turned to Mary and grabbed her hand and moved her to the center of the room. Victory then retrieved the pedestal and went to Mary motioning her to lay down. She looked at the men and they gave her encouraging looks so she laid on the floor. Victory then lifted the pedestal and pretended to swing in right down on Mary's pelvis. Mary flinched but was relieved to find herself unharmed, but felt around her to make sure she was all there. Victory threw the pedestal across the room she was done with it, she pointed to her own pelvis and that was what Doc had been waiting for. He knew what she was doing and what it was done for. The pieces were finally beginning to come together. Now if only they could find this Man. Doc told Victory that he was going to give her some medicine that would make her sleepy and her hurting stomach will go away. She nodded as she closely hovered over the old man as he reached into his bag. When he went to the pitcher she followed him watching his every move closely. She watched as he took a small bottle of white powder out of his bag and a little spoon. Doc carefully measured the medicine out and put it into a cup of water. He swished it around a bit before handing it to Victory. She sniffed and swished it round. It didn't look to appealing and she wasn't sure she wanted to drink it. "Go ahead and take it, it won't hurt you I promise", Black said to try and influence her to drink it. She took the glass and after a few minutes of her getting up the courage she drank it down and almost vomited from the taste.

Mary got the night shirt and helped Victory put it on as Doc started to gather up is tools of the trade and put them back in his bag. Victory however had other plans as she jumped up and took the top most blanket that the tools sat on and wrapped them up to deposit them in the bottom of her wardrobe. Wiping her hands clean she got back into bed and with a smile on his face Black tucked her in like he had since the first night she was here.

Doc motioned Black to the door, "it will take a bit for the medicine to work." Let us know Mary when she is asleep." Mary nodded and sat in the chair next to the bed as the men left the room to an anxious group of men in the hallway. "Well did you make progress? What did you learn? Is she alright? What was all that noise in there?" Black had to smile if only they had seen her naked and her little self-breaking up that table. It was a sight one he won't soon forget.

Black was tired it has been a long day and it had to be well past midnight now. They all sat in the hall awaiting one last step; Doc had sedated her so that he could examine her without her knowing or even caring. He also mix a little pain medication for the stomach ailment.   After a few relaxing minutes Mary opened the door and motions that she was asleep. Doc stood and Black stood to follow, Doc put his hand up and told him that this wasn't something that he needed to be there for and to just rest it wouldn't take long.

After about an hour Doc emerged from the room wiping his hands on a towel. Doc looked old as he stepped out into the hall way. Most of them men were dosing until they heard the door open. Mary was behind him extinguishing the oil lamp by the door. Doc sat down on the hall bench and Black sat beside him. The men woke and gathered around as Doc told them that she would be fine she was going to sleep the night away and would be back to herself by morning. The men seemed to be satisfied with the news and said there good nights as they went their separate ways. All but Richard and Mary they were hoping that everyone would go so they could spend some time together. But it became apparent that Doc had more to tell Black.

He looked at Richard and Mary and Black decided they might as well here what Doc had to say.

"Well let's first back track on what we *do* know. It would seem that the rumors are true; it's a doctor who is heading up this secret society. From the state of Victory's scars they were made by someone who knew what they were doing. The purpose of what he did is still unclear. We know that she did have a family but I wouldn't even know where to begin." Black started to think, "well we know Mama, Papa and Ricky. Maybe we could start going door to door asking everyone if they are Mama, Papa or Ricky." They all had a laugh at the thought. Richard asked why they were calling her Victory now; Doc explained what they had learned about her name. "She said her name was Victory although I still wonder if we haven't miss heard."

Richard suddenly fell to his knees with his hands covering his face, "Did you say Victory, Mama, Papa, and Ricky?" They all looked at each other, "what are you trying to say Richard." "Ricky is my... well the name my parents call me, *my Mama and Papa*. Richard sat there in silence for a few moments while he gathered his thoughts and tried to make since of what was happening. When I was three I had a twin sister, we use to sleep together because she was afraid of the dark. One night my parents made me sleep in another room, they said that my sister was sick and that the doctor was coming to check on her.

I went to bed in the spare room that night and never saw my sister again. My parents said she became very ill and the doctor took her to his hospital where she died. He sent her home in her casket and he told my parents not to open it because she had a sickness that could still spread. She is still buried there to this day or at least we all thought she was. My sister's name is Victoria but she loved to race around and when she was learning to talk we would race and she would try to say her name when she hit the finish line she would yell what sounded like Victory so we started calling her that.

"Gods blood man do you know what this means." Black said as he shot up from his chair. Doc shot up to the implication of the possibilities. "Tell me Richard do you remember what your sister looked like." He bowed his head, "no, it was too long ago and we were only three." "What about a mark, a scar, something that could identify her without a doubt." Richard was thinking so hard that he was sure there was steam coming from his head. "If my memory serves me right one day we were playing and I knocked off a tea cup from the table and broke it. Victory came running to see what the noise was and slipped and cut her knee on a few pieces. When it healed my mother said she had her own cross on her knee." With that they quickly but quietly entered the room and made their way to the bed. Black pulled down the blanket trying not to disturb the sleeping girl, if she woke who knows what she would think or do. Doc pulled her night shirt up just above her knees. Do you know which knee it would be on?" Richard shook his head; no it was too long ago to remember. Doc searched and after a good look there it was right above her right knee. A small scar that looked like a little cross he almost missed it because it was higher than he was originally looking.

Doc put the covers back and Black covered his sleeping beauty, and gave her a soft kiss on her forehead before they all left the room. This act didn't go unnoticed by Mary. She gave her brother a good look. His face is hard again just like before. You can see the worry and hurt on him. Her brother for all of her love for him would

never be enough as it is with this woman.
He loved her, You could see it in his eyes, in
his pain and in his need to heal her and
keep her safe. Her brother the one she
never thought would find love, has found it
and it is the hardest kind of love. Yet, here
he is, in love with this woman, who has
really never even said a word to him.

As they all stepped out of the room
Richard stepped back in and took a good
look at her sleeping form. Black came to
stand next to him and put his hand on his
shoulder. "I can't believe she has been alive
this whole time. And to think what she
must of have gone through. I just feel like I
want to kill someone for this, you know,
make someone pay. Yet, I'm so happy it's
like a piece of me has been put back in my

heart." Richard declared as he turned and looked at Black. "I know and now we can start the healing," he replied.

Mary and Richard walked off to their rooms dazed and confused about all that has happened. Doc and Black were left in the hallway alone. Doc turned to Black and put his hand on his shoulder, "well my son I'm afraid your night isn't over yet. Let's go to your office there is something we need to talk about and some decisions that need to be made. Black was in a whirlwind of thought, now that he knew who she belonged to she would be going. Leaving him to go back to the life she should of always had. This thought process made Black very angry, his jaw set and brow wrinkled at the thought of losing her.

The two men entered the office; Black went right for the liquor cabinet as Doc followed behind and closed the door. Doc accepted a drink from Black and they both sat in silence for a bit, letting it all sink in. A lot to think about. But Doc broke the silence by telling Black that her parents needed to be notified as soon as possible. They both agreed that Black would write a note to Richards's parents and have Richard deliver it and bring them here. But yet Black was down about the fact that she would be leaving to be with her parents.

"Black you know you are like a son to me, you know that your happiness matters as well. But there is something you need to know. First let me tell you that I know you have been with Victory." Blacks head shot up, and then a look of shame over took him. "And I as well as everyone can see you love her very much." Black lowered his head and shook it. It was something he has never really admitted before now. "That transparent am I?" Black said as he brushed his hand through his hair. Doc took a deep breath and began to tell him the hardest news he would have had to give. "Adrian, she is with child." With that he spun around, "WHAT!" He had a look of a wild man as his mind played the news over and over. "What a fool I am," he thought. The thought of pregnancy never entered his mind. "I ruined her and got her with child, I am the very scum that I hate the most."

Doc jumped up and quickly added, "Don't be so hard on yourself she is a beautiful woman and you love her very much. It just happened, and you are supposed to be together, everyone can see it. She loves you Black and you love her." Doc stopped and his head went down like he just was hit with a brick in the head. "Black I'm afraid that's not the bad news. She can't bear a child. Her pelvis has been broken like the other women in a way that when it heals they cannot pass a child thru. I am sorry Black but she needs to lose the baby and quickly or it will be a death sentence for her." Tears formed in the corner of Blacks eyes, this was too much, too much to handle in one night. Doc was worried for Black he has always been a strong man with strong convictions. Now all this, the poor lad finally falls in love and all this has to go with it.

Black paced the floor silently for a bit. He was hurt, how could he have done this to her. He killed her. After all she had been through in her life and it was him that kills her. Well not on his watch, "how do we get rid of the baby." "I have medicines that will take care of it. It's for the best Black, our medicines and knowledge is just not advanced enough to help her. Black bowed his head; he was beat he couldn't take anymore. A baby…….. They had made a baby together and now he has to kill it. How will he tell Victory? Doc put his hand on his shoulder. "You don't have to think about it anymore tonight, we will talk again in the morning." With that Doc left the room, his heart heavy for the man that has always been like a son to him, and because of this burden he now has to carry.

Black sat in his office drinking away the night. He watched as the fire in the fireplace dance an uncaring dance before his eyes. God he wished his father and mother were here to help him. But his train of thought told him that they would not have approve of him sleeping with his ward. "Damn" Black said to himself how could I have stooped so low as to not only take my wards virginity but get her with child. Black knew he would never forgive himself for this. And now he was the cause of his only child's death.

The next morning Mary and Doc found Black in his office sitting at his desk. He was working on papers as he normally did; he looked up and told them morning as if all was as it should be. Doc filled Marry in on the situation so she was confused as to why he was acting like nothing was wrong. She stood before the large desk; he looked up with paper in mid hand as if she had interrupted something. Her brother was different this morning. Hard as stone even more so then she had ever seen him. Mary became instantly sad for her him cause she knew his heart was breaking. And that he was probably punishing himself.

Adrian? Black, looked her in the eyes with a cold hard stair. "Call Richard in here, I have prepared a dispatch to be sent to his parents. Call the men together we need to organize everything for the search for the animal Victory calls Man." He started to rattle off another request and Mary couldn't take it anymore. With tears in her eyes she ran around the desk to her brother and thru her arms around his neck. He didn't move at first. Then as sternly as she had ever seen, he reached up and unfolded her arms from around his neck to set her aside. In almost and in audio voice with his head down he said, "Now is not the time for the nonsense of childish girls, go and check on our ward." Doc raised his hand as he was about to say something, Black cut him off abruptly, "No Don't". He stopped him from talking. But not Mary she was going to let him have it. "How could you just turn your back on her, she loves you and you love her. Arrie why are you being so cold? I thought…….. I thought…." "You thought what Mary that we would get married and live happily ever after, wake up Mary this is the real world. What I did is inexcusable and now she is the one who has to pay for my inability to keep it to myself." " Oh God no Addie there is nothing wrong with you loving her, please Addie don't do this."

 "Don't do what the right thing, this is the right thing. Doc is going to take care of the problem and she will be returned to her family, END OF STORY!" "Addie wait shouldn't she be told about the baby. Shouldn't she know what you plan for her for the both of you? You will break her heart Addie can't you see that." With that he looked at his sister with pity. "Fine we will tell her and you will see in the real world Mary she will hate me for what I have done to her." Mary smiled triumphantly she won this round and he will see that she loves him.

Richard walked into the office as Mary and Doc were leaving. Richard and Mary exchanged looks that told Richard to watch out her brother was on the war path. But what Richards saw when he looked at Black he was not prepared for. Their eyes made contact and Black quickly turned away, Richard almost thought he looked ashamed of something.

Black handed him a parchment from this desk. "Richard this is a letter to your parents telling them what has happened to a certain extent, we can spare them the gory details I think for their own piece of mind. I want you to fetch your parents so they can be reunited with their daughter. But first we need to go tell Victory of this new development. She will be happy to know she has a family again." Richard nodded confused as to the way Back was acting. He was short and almost detached from everything.

Together they walked up the stairs to victory's room where they found Mary and Doc all talking up a storm. Victory saw Black as he walked in and new right away something was wrong with him. He seemed distant from her like he wouldn't look at her. Then fear welled up inside of her, Oh my god he is disgusted by me. He found out where I'm from and he is sickened by the very thought of me. But before she could think any more on it Doc startled her by say, "Victoria we have some news for you and I think you will be happy about it." They looked at Black expectantly thinking he would want to tell her the news about her brother and family. Instead he backed away and looked down. Mary piped up happily to tell her the great news.

"Victoria we have found your family." Her eyes widened and she looked like she was about to choke in a good way. She propped up on her knees in bed and they all looked at Richard who was smiling by now. He came forth and sat in the chair next to the bed. The others left the room so

Richard could explain to her about his missing sister.

Richard looked at Victory and smiled. "Many years ago when I was three I had a sister. She became sick and the doctors took her away to hospital. They said she died and they sent her body home to be buried in the family plot. We buried her and it devastated us, until now. You see my sister didn't really die as we thought; she was taken from us by the doctor who was supposed to help her. That's you Victory, you are my sister. I am Ricky and Mama and Pa are going to be fetched today so we can all be together." He waited for some response positive or not he didn't care just something, some kind of reaction.

She sat their momentarily in shock her mouth wide open. Then she seemed to regain some memory in her mind. As Richard stood she flung herself into his arms. And they both fell to the floor, Richard holding her and Victory holding him. Hugging and crying it was the happiest day of their lives. She kept looking at him hugging him, as if she was waiting for it to be a joke. Till finally, "well we better go tell the others, and I am going to fetch mom and dad, it will take a few days. So I better get going." She sat there on the floor staring at him she didn't want to let min out of her sight. All these years she was told they were dead. And all along she had a family a real family. This is the happiest day of her life. She has a family and Black, what

more could she ever want. Then Richard
deposited her on her bed and told her she
needed rest and brushed her cheek with a
gentle kiss. He left the room and Victory
became sullen and realized that Black didn't
seem to want to be around her anymore.
She thought she couldn't blame he couldn't
love her with the life she had and the
scaring she had. But it still hurt to think
that she lost the only man she loved.

Chapter 6

Later that day Black was confronted by Doc and Mary. "You need to tell her about the baby Black. It really does need to come from you. I will tell her if you want, but she love you."

Black sighed, "Where is she?" Resigned to the fact, that she would hate him, and blame him for everything. "In her usual haunt"? He nodded and walked off. As he neared the chapel doors he slowed, this was the worst moment of his life. He slowly opened the door and slowly walked up the isle to her pew in the front. He sat down next to her. She didn't look at him, this was it, and this is where he tells her she is going home away from him. And, never to see him again. The thought stabbed her like a knife and it was a pain so bad that it hurt more than anything Man could have done to her.

Black glanced a look at their and saw she was staring at him waiting for him to speak. Her face was pale with all the new information she needed to digest and now he was fixing to throw her a blow that will seal both hers and his fate.

He shyly and softly grabbed her hand, momentarily staring at the perfection of her fingers entwined in his. "Victory…. He paused, while you were a sleep the Doctor looked you over to make sure you weren't hurt. He knows we made love. "Her head fell and she looked down ashamed all of a sudden. "This is it, this is why he will send me away, because I wanted to make love to him." Black took a deep breath and started again. "Doc says……..well he said….. Victoria…. Catherine I mean Victory." He was getting frustrated now. "Shit!" "Victory ….. You are pregnant. Do you understand that, you know what that means?" She looked at him blankly in shock, but she understood very well what he was saying. "A baby, victory you have a baby in side of you. One that we made, when we made love." She looked down, her mind really in thought. She was pregnant with Blacks baby. Did he not want to have a baby with her? Is he so disgusted that he is going to cast the two of them out.

Black looked down and added, "I'm sorry Victory, I did this to you." Doc said that with the condition of your bones you can't have a baby. It will kill you. I'm sorry." She sat stock still for a moment as the thought process when thru her mind. Then it hit her what he was talking about . The other girls at the Man's place, a chill went through her as she thought of what happened to them. But Black loved her.

Victoria was confused; did he want her to leave? Did he want her to get rid of this baby so he could send her on her way? Her heart was breaking with every thought. She couldn't look at him, didn't want to look at him. Did he hate her that much?

Black could see she was in turmoil with every expression on her face. He couldn't help but hurt for her, he loved her and now she sees what kind of man he is. She is disgusted by what he did to her. If only there was a way to make this all go away, back to the way things were.

A tear escaped Blacks eye, he isn't the crying type but it seems that the last twenty four hours life has thrown him so many heart aches. He didn't keep it in check he didn't care anymore. He didn't care if he lived or died. He had no will to live without his Victoria. And he can see the anger building in her eyes as she realizes what he has done.

Victoria stole a glance out of the corner of her eye at Black. Only to turn her head in amazement, he was crying. What was he crying about? What was he thinking? Is it possible that he does love her? She looked at him almost with anger in her eyes. She thought to her self how stupid he was being. She wanted him just as much as he wanted her. She new what pregnancy would do to her, all the young woman dying in agony not being able to give birth until the Man said it was time.

She lifted her hand and placed her palm on his cheek and gently wiped his tear with her thumb. She looked into his eyes, trying to convey what she was thinking, willing him to understand all that she can't say but is thinking. She wants him to see that she loves him more than herself. His happiness meant everything to her. She couldn't take it anymore; she jumped up and ran out skirting Blacks legs. He let her go, he knew what she was running from, him.

And she did run, she rain right to the barn where Milles puppies were. She flopped on the ground in their little pen, letting her tears flow unchecked into the soft fur of the puppies. And there, she cried and cried.

Black sat in the pew for what seemed hours. He was making himself mad with the beating he was giving himself. He has himself believing that he was the worst kind of person. He was lower than dirt. After a long while Black lifted himself off the pew. He felt old, he felt like every bone in his body was breaking. Every muscle ached including his heart.

Chapter 7

The day wore on with the house in total silence. Everyone was walking on egg shells. Black was in a dark place and no one wanted to get in his path. Until Mary who was undisturbed by his moods, walked in to his office where he sat that evening with his drink at his desk. His brooding eyes fixed on the papers on his desk until he looked up and saw Mary. Mary stood in front of his desk, she had, had enough of this poor me crap her brother was putting himself thru. She took her hand and angrily swiped all the contents of the deck onto the floor. Oh yah she was mad, if he wanted to act like a child she would either act like one too or treat him like one. Two can play this game.

"Brother your self-loathing is disgusting me. Why don't you get off your ass and talk to her. Tell her how you fell. Why must you insist on being like this? I suggest if you love her you tell her and we can all move on from there. If you think I am going to pussy foot around my own home to keep you from getting angry then your sadly mistaken. My Lord Black if you are going to throw away your chance at happiness then fine, however you are not taking us all with you. Also you might as well know that me and Richard are in love and we plan to marry so you can either be happy for us or not I really don't care at this point. I love him and we have been secretly courting for over a year. And because of your hard headedness we have kept it a secret because Richard was afraid you would kill him if he asked for my hand. So get use to the idea, If you want to suffer in some self-made prison that's fine, but I am going to be happy with or without you." There she said it, she let him have it. She turned and stormed out of the room.

Richard waited just down the hall. They all have been trying to stay back but Mary wasn't going to let true love be stopped by a hard head. And her brother could have a very hard head. Mary literally stomped out of the office making sure he understood her point. In the hall way stood Richard, he had heard everything and was wowed by her bravery. Mary gave him a humph look and smiled the biggest smile she could. Turned and went on her way. "God I love this women". Richard smiled and turned and headed the other way.

Black sat in his office dumb struck, Richard and Mary? Wow he had no idea. And she sure let him have it. Black swished the whiskey in his glass. Maybe Mary is right; maybe it's all in his head. He thought about it for a while, deep in thought he was as Doc entered the office.

"Son you know I want your happiness to its full extent but…." Black put his hand up and stopped him in mid-sentence. Why is everyone so intent on my happiness? Black stood and slammed his hands on his desk, he's had enough of this. Fine if everyone wanted him to try to work it out with Victoria than fine he will go talk to her and then everyone will see.

Black stormed out of the room and headed right for Victoria's room. He wanted to put this all behind him. He stormed into Victoria's room; he wasn't angry he was more worried that his fears would be confirmed. He was happy beating himself up without having to face weather it was the truth or not. It was just easier this way.

So, their he stood in the middle of her room. But it was dark, and cold, she wasn't in there. The sun is setting and the lamps are not lit yet and her night clothes haven't been put out. A shock of fear ran thru him. He spun around and ran to the hall way. "Where the hell is Victoria". He yelled. Several doors in the hall way opened. And heads peered down the hallway, everyone started to gather from all over the house. Black became frantic because no one seemed to know where she was. And no one saw her leave, Black barked out orders sending the men scattering thru the house to find her. Black himself ran to the chapel where she seemed to always be. It was dark and empty. Black turned on a start and ran to the hall way checking every room and every nook and cranny. No one could find her; Black was out of places to look.

"Did she leave him already? Where would she have gone?" Black went to the garden, nothing, he went to the horse barn, nothing. His heart sank and his fear welled up inside of him. "Was she kidnapped?" Fear turned to anger, "Did the Man find her and take her back. Oh God no, please no." His heart was racing he started running from place to place. He swung open the stock barn door. And ran in, checking every stall, his breath quickening his chest hurting. Just then in the last stall a little wine from the new litter of puppies. He ran to the stall and there, she was curled up asleep lined with a mess of sleeping puppies. Black swung open the gate to the stall and grabbed up Victoria in his arms.

She woke with a start to Black crushing her to him. It was a desperate hold on her. He put on her feet pulled her away and quickly checked her for any damage. He was so happy to have found her that he didn't even notice the tears pouring down his face. Victoria wiped away his tears and stared at him in wonder. She didn't understand what the fuss was. Black kissed her, he frantically kissed her cheek and her forehead and her chin and her nose.

Victoria's heart swelled he did love her she knew it. She hugged him and hugged him. Black picked her up and carried her back to the house. As he walked into the parlor everyone came running. For over an hour everyone has been looking for the missing girl. "Where was she?" Mary frantically asked. In all the hustle Victoria still had a big grin on her face. He loved her was all she needed to know.

With the relief of finding Victoria Mary took her to her room, where Victoria could wash up and freshen up before they went down to a much deserved late dinner.

After they cleaned up and donned clean dresses Mary sat on Victoria's bed and patted the spot next to her and Victoria sat. Mary gave her a big hug and then let her go with a scolding, "you know you gave everyone quite the scare." Victoria looked down she felt bad for scaring everyone. But she needed to be alone with her grief.

Now she just wanted to see Black again, he loved her and she loved him that was all that mattered now.

At dinner everyone sat and ate in silence. Nobody was able to judge Blacks mood. He seemed with drawn he ate and drank but didn't look up. Victoria sat in normal seat next to Mary and silently at. But she couldn't help but have a little grin on her face. Everything was going to work out she thought, it just had to.

Mary couldn't stand it anymore this was ridiculous to keep on like this. Mary clanged her fork and knife together and slammed them down on the table. She got up from the table gave everyone a look of disgust and stormed out. Victoria just looked after her. "Wow everyone seems to be in a mood not just Black." Victoria looked at Black from down the table. She stood and grabbed her plate and glass and casually as if all was normal, walked to the seat next to Black who was at the head of the table. She looked him in the eye he was brooding and she hates his brooding so she whipped out her best and brightest smile. Black just stared at her blankly. He was dumb struck as to what to do or say to her. So he did the next best thing and smiled back at her.

He relaxed a bit and took Victoria's hand in his and now was the time to hit this head on. Time was running out for her and he didn't want to take a chance anymore. Not with her life. "Victoria I don't want any harm come to you ever. When we couldn't find you I thought the worst for you. We need to talk or, well I need to talk. We have to do something about the baby. We can't wait any longer I don't want to lose you."

Victoria Smiled, their, he didn't say he loved her but he got pretty close. "Doc can take care of it and I will be with you every step of the way. This is for the best Victoria." She looked at him, she was deep in thought now, she hadn't gotten much past the idea that he was trying to get rid of her. Now they are talking about the baby, their baby, one they made together. Would she be able to kill her own child? There has to be another way.

Victoria put her palm on his cheek to tell him that she was listening. Then she stood and walked to him and plopped herself down on his lap and hugged him. He hugged her tight. She looked at him and with much surprise to Black she said, "Baby." Black just about jump from his seat, she talked and she talked clearly. Victoria took his hand and put it on her belly. And said, "Ours". He nodded, "yes ours but we have to or you will die, I can't handle that Victoria." "Ours", she said and gave him a look that told him that she wasn't wanting to do it. She couldn't get rid of something so beautiful.

Black had a stab of fear. She didn't want to get rid of the baby. How was he going to make her understand that it was for her safety. "Please Victoria; you know why it has to be done, why we have to give it up. I would rather have you alive and childless and not at all." She gave him a gentle kiss and looked him in the eye and smiled. It was a smile that said I understand why but I can't, I love you but this baby is ours and I'm not giving it up." He pleaded with her to no avail she wasn't going to do it at least not right now." His heart sank.

After dinner Black went in search of Doc, maybe there was another way. He found Doc in the parlor and approached him cautiously. Sitting in the chair next to him she gave a sigh to let Doc know he wanted to talk. "So…. What's on your mind young man," Doc asked. "Victoria wants to keep the baby; I don't know what to do Doc?" "I guess the only thing left is to plan a wedding hey." Black looked at him, how could he be so casual about this. And a wedding he never thought about marriage. He wasn't against it he just hadn't thought of it. "Doc, you said she would die if she kept this baby I can't go thru what little life we would have together if she keeps it knowing that she wouldn't survive." "Black, that young woman of yours has been to hell and back. Now she has a chance to love and be loved no matter how short it is. My guess is death doesn't really mean to her what it means to us. She lived everyday with death she is ready for it. And this baby is a part of her. A part of her that she can give you to love and raise in a happy home. Something she never remembers having. So I can't blame her for wanting to keep it. Can you?"

Black was flabbergasted he didn't know what to think. Of course he could understand why she wanted to keep it damn he wanted it too. But he would rather have her ....ALIVE. He was at a loss he didn't know what to do and a panic has started to rise in his thought.

"Black there might be another way." He had Blacks attention now. "There is an experimental way to deliver a baby. I have never done it nor have I seen it done. But they take the baby thru the abdomen and that would work perfect for Victoria. I will have to do some research. I have a fellow doctor in Wilshire who knows about this procedure. I will contact him and see what he says, it the best chance for her."

Black now had some hope that this could work out for the best. Now, came the thought of marriage. He never saw himself as the marring type. But he now knows he wants Victoria as his wife. He has no doubt about that. He made his way from the parlor to Victoria's room only to find she wasn't there. He was ready to wake the whole house when his door across the hall creaked open and their stood Victoria. She peaked out of his room when she heard him.

He covered the spans of space between him in just a few strides. Reaching her at the door he grabbed her and held her. Smelling her rose sent, and her soft body against his. She was in her night shirt which meant she wanted to stay in his room tonight. And he was more than happy to oblige her. He kissed her deeply as she thru her head back so he had better access to her neck which he kissed hungrily. He dipped his hand down her side, her outer thigh down her leg a bit and then slowly as he kissed her neck he lifted her night dress till her bare bottom what under his hand. He couldn't take it, this woman drove him mad with want. He stopped suddenly and picked her up and quickly deposited her on the bed. He looked down on her as he hastily undressed. She was so beautiful, her long dark hair flowing on his pillow, her lips full from his kisses. God he loved her! After he undressed he spread out beside her, kissing her everywhere and taking in her sent. He lifted her leg and placed it on his hip and she now she was facing him. Until she popped herself up and swung her leg over his as he laid on his back. She straddled him and was smiling because she now felt she was in control. But Black wanted her to much at this moment to wait any longer. He flipped her onto her back and with a wicked smile he penetrated her. Victoria's head tilted back from the pure luxury of the feel of him in side of her. She needed him, and he needed her. They climaxed together and Black collapsed on top of her. Careful, not to crush her.

He rested his head in curve of her neck, he loved the way she smells like a garden at full bloom. He rolled on his side so he could see her and propped himself up on his elbow. "Victoria are you sure you want to have this baby, even with the chances that you might not make it?" He looked at her intently trying to gage her reaction. She nodded yes and smiled an, all will be alright smile. Black kissed her and rolled on his back and said with a laugh, "Well the only thing left is to get married, guess we better call the preacher." She turned and looked at him with surprise this was unexpected and she was in shock. As the realization hit her what he was saying she turned and jumped on him and kissed him! He could tell she was happy about it. Black decided that if they were going to do this than he was going to make her the happiest he could in the short time they might have together. All the things she missed out on growing up she was now going to experience. And Black had a plan for the first of her experiences.

One warm morning a week later Black found Victoria and Mary in the Parlor with the dress maker. Mary was barking out orders while Victoria stood arms out and a look of sheer misery on her face. They decided to make this a quick wedding in Victoria's beloved chapel. The Father however is out of town for three weeks. So Mary took it upon herself to order the wedding dress made and plan the service. She was so happy and excited about this whole thing. Mary hasn't talked to Black about her and Richard since that day in the office. She wasn't scared she was just waiting for the right time to approach the subject. Black stood and watched the women working and all the fluttering around that they were doing when he heard a carriage coming up the drive.

Black went out to the steps to find Richards family dismounting from the carriage. The moment had come for Victoria to meet her parents again. By the look of them the shock has worn off into anticipation. Black shook hands with Richard and gave him a smile of hidden meaning. He gave Richard some quick orders and smiled and went back into the house. The ladies where just finishing up with the dress prep as Black walked in and motioned to Mary to come over there. He told her that Victoria's parent were here and to take her up to her room while he settles her parents.

So excited, Mary almost squealed with excitement. She went and told Victoria they needed to get ready for lunch. So the two women went upstairs just as Richard and his parents entered. Sir Holloway and his wife Lady Holloway have been long time friends of the Blacks. After exchanging welcomes Black and Richard lead the couple to the parlor were everyone was served tea. Black watched as Lady Holloway would glance at the doors, he could tell she wanted her daughter to arrive.

Up in Mary's room the girls washed and dressed for lunch. Victoria returned to her room because Mary told her Black would be coming to get her for lunch. Victoria paced in her room for what she felt was hours but only minutes when there came a knock on the door. She turned and Richard peered in the room. She ran to him and gave him a big smile and met him halfway to give him a big hug. "Hey sis I'm sorry it took so long but…. Just as he said that their came another knock at the door and Black came in Victoria's smile got even bigger with the sight of him. But behind him following him into the room were two older well-dressed people. Richard grabbed Victoria's hand and leaned in and quietly announced this is Mama and Papa Victoria. Her head shot up and she stood there and stared at the tall man and woman standing in front of her.

Victoria wavered a bit and almost lost her footing with the shock. All these years she was told they were dead and here they are right in front of her. Her own Mother and Father. She was paralyzed with excitement, sadness and anger all in one for all the wasted time. Tears started to flow out of her eyes unchecked. Her mother was the first to move, holding out her arms to Victoria with tears of her own flowed.

Victoria went right to her almost running into her arms. The new family almost collapsed on the floor in a great family hug. Everyone was in tears by now. Black grabbed Mary's arm who had walked in on the going ons and led her from the room closing the door behind them so the family can have some time alone.

As Mary and Black walked down the hall she stopped him in mid step and gave him a big hug. See Lord Black everything is going to work out. She gave him a smile before adding, "Maybe we should make this a double wedding." She looked at him waiting expectantly. Black stood still and it made Mary nervous that he was taking so long to answer her. "Addie I love him, I love him very much and he wants to make me his wife. Please Addie you know I will marry him with or without you." He had no doubt of it. Black thru his head back and gave the biggest roaring laugh she had ever heard from him. She didn't know if this was good or bad. Black grabbed up Mary in a big bear hug, "of course Mary you can marry Richard. He is already family anyways. And if you want to make this a double wedding I'm all for it, but you have to ask Victoria if she will share her special day with you."

"Oh Addie I love you so much." With that

they went down to lunch all smiles in the house today, Black was happy and content for the first time in his life.

As the two sat in the big dining room waiting for the other guests Black decided to talk to Mary about Victoria keeping the baby. "Victoria has decided come what may she was keeping the baby." "No Addie she can't it will kill her." "Doc is on a mission to find a friend he knows that has a way of delivering a baby thru the abdomen." Mary was dumb struck; she didn't know what to say. "Mary I want you to be close to her as much as possible doing this time to help keep an eye on her. Can I count on you for this?" "Of course Addie anything I love Victoria, I sure hope Doc finds what he is looking for, For Victoria's and your sake."

With that the Holloways entered the room the proud father with his newly discovered daughter on his arm. Everyone took a seat and lunch was served. There wasn't much talking going on everyone quite overwhelmed. After lunch everyone went to the parlor and took seats. Richard started to explain that when he got home an broke the news his father had the Victoria's grave dug up and what they found shocked them all. It wasn't the remains of their beloved daughter but that of a dog. Black asked, if they knew the doctor who took Victoria to the hospital. Lord Holloway told Black that is was Dr Hans from Germany, but he had died years ago. As the men talked in detail to try and put some information together. Black did find out that Dr. Hans had a son who live not far from the Black estate. Black knew of this man but never met him. He was a hermit as far as he knew. The Father who was coming to do the weddings was actually the over seer of that estates chapel. Father Browning has been a family friend for years and was due back in a week or so. Black thought he might be able to get some information about the family from him.

Then the talk went to Black and Victoria's wedding, now Black was in the hot seat and about to be confronted by her parents. He now has a good idea about what Richard felt and could sympathize with him. It was hard to be on this side of the receiving end for him. Black cleared his throat and stood up, "Lord Holloway may I have a moment of your time." Black asked with more confidence than he felt. "Lord Black you may, shall we convene in your office." The two men got up and left the room. Victoria watched the men as they left, not understanding what they were going to talk about.

As Black led him to the office he could feel his palms sweat. What if he said no! Oh shit, he never thought of the possibility of him disapproving of them getting married. As they entered the office Black took his seat behind the desk, he just felt more comfortable there. He motioned for Lord Holloway to sit as he jumped up and got them a drink. "Lord Holloway, I don't know how much Richard has told you."

Lord Holloway lifted his hand, "he told my

enough, my question to you Lord Black is do

you love my daughter? I only had her back

for a few hours and now I know you are

going to ask for Victoria's hand. Richard

told me all about it. I am not a man of

many words you know that Black, But I am

in debt to you for giving me back my

daughter. Her happiness is the most

important thing to me now. I guess what I

am trying to say Black is I would be proud to

have you marry my daughter." "However

there is one thing I would like to ask in

return, and that's that we, my wife and I

may come and go as we wish. So, that we

can spend time with Victoria and Richard of

course."

Of course Black agreed full heartedly he wouldn't of had it any other way. And that was part of his plan for Victoria to experience a childhood. Black and Victoria's father talked for a while longer about the captivity of Victoria, but Black was very careful not to tell them to much, it would hurt the poor man to know just what she went thru. After a while the men rejoined everyone in the parlor, where Mary was playing the harp and Victoria was leaning on her mother's shoulder in perfect content. Her father came to sit on the other side of her; Victoria took his arm in hers as she leaned against her mother.

Black took a seat across from them and next to Richard. That way he could enjoy the beautiful sight of their soon to be brides.

Chapter 8

Black sat in his office one morning when a knock came to the door. Richard entered the room. Oh great here we go again Black thought. He knew why he was here. Black thought about how just a few days earlier he had that same look on his face. "Ummm

Black, I was wonder if I could have a word with you." "Come in Richard what can I help you with?" "Well umm since you already know about me and Mary I was wondering, I mean, If it's all right with you, I mean if I could have your permission to marry your sister." Black sat back in his chair, a smile creeping across his face. He liked being on this side of the conversation. But he felt for poor Richard and decided not to keep him waiting any longer for his love. "Richard, I have known you for how long now? Never mind it really doesn't matter. Richard we have been together for a long time. I would be honored for you to marry my sister." Richard let out a breath; he didn't even know he was holding. Within seconds Mary came barging in. "Addie don't you go to hard on him you already said we could." "Mary we already talked it's a done deal." Black smiled at her and Richard now you two get out of my office so I can get some work done." After they left Black couldn't help but give a small laugh at the whole thing.

Over the next week everyone got into a nice routine around the house. The parents spent as much time with Victoria as they could. Black often found them sitting in the Chapel trying to teach Victoria to talk. It was another experience she got to have of growing up. She also learned to ride a horse and fell a few times playing ball with Crons kids and skinned her knee. Black laugh at her because when a child skins their knee they usually cry she laughed.

At the end of the week Father Browning came by. Him and Black talked along time in his office. He was happy for the Blacks to have finally found love. He agreed to perform the wedding this coming weekend. Father Browning was in a hurry so he didn't get a chance to meet Victoria since she was out with Richard for her riding lesson. He promised to spend some time with her the day of the wedding. With that Father Browning left promising to return the next weekend for the nuptials.

One night Black heard Victoria's bed chamber door opening. He waited for her to enter as she usually did. They had been however lately staying in their own rooms since her parents were down the hall. Black waited but nothing, then he heard the door to her parent's room open and close. Black laid back and smiled experience number……. Well who knows but he laid back and smiled to himself.

Victoria didn't want to sleep in the dark so she sneaked into her parent's room to their surprise. She crawled into bed between them, climbed under the blanket and snuggled to her mom. She loved it and every night until the wedding that's where you could find her.

The morning of the wedding came and the whole house was moving quickly. Black decided not to invite anyone except his men at arms. This way Victoria will feel comfortable. Mary and Victoria Readied themselves in Mary's room. The maids and

the two women did hair and picked out
jewelry and helped each other. It was a
wonderful day for the two. Father
Browning went to the girls room to visit
with them for a while. When he arrived
there they were dressed and were just
waiting for the que to go. Mary introduced
Victoria to Father Browning. He was taken
by her beauty. Black had told him she was a
mute so he wouldn't ask to many questions.
But the poor Father was so enchanted by
her beauty that her shyness didn't seem to
matter to him. He scooted closer to
Victoria and put his hand on her knee.
Victoria didn't like him. She felt bad, she
didn't she wanted this to be over with.
After a lengthy visit with the Father the
time came to make their way to the Chapel.

Victoria's father came to get them. It was agreed that since Black was getting married he couldn't walk his sister down the aisle so Lord Holloway got the honor of walking the ladies down the aisle.

The ceremony was short and sweet. After the wedding everyone gathered in a garden for wonderfully prepared dinner. It was a perfect night for the dinner. Black just wanted it to be over, he didn't like all the attention. Early on Father Browning bid his good lucks and farewells. By evening Mary and Richard were saying their good byes, they would leave in the morning for London for a few weeks. Black and Victoria decided to stay home for their honeymoon. Victoria was quite happy to stay home.

Everyone bid their fond farewells to the two couples and wishes of luck. Richard and Mary retired to their room. Black, and Victoria to theirs. When they entered Blacks room she noticed her night shirt was laid out on his bed. When she looked in his wardrobe she saw that all her things had been brought over to his room. Black was concerned for Victoria, she looked tired; he hoped that the day wasn't too much for her. He undressed her slowly taking time to kiss everywhere he could. As her dress dropped to the floor he got down on his knees and kissed her gently on the belly. She now has a little bump growing. He rose up to take time on each bare breast first one then the other. Taking the nipples in his mouth and suckling gently. He took her

to their bed and laid her down; he quickly
undressed and lay next to her. Taking his
time, to love his new wife from head to toe.

He bent down and positioned himself
between her thighs. He wanted to taste
her; he loved her taste that was hers alone.
As he lavished on her woman's place
Victoria's head was back and swaying side
to side with the on slot of his tongue. She
was peeking he could feel it in her muscles.
But he didn't want her to climax yet so he
stopped his on slot of her woman's spot.
He kneeled inside her thighs as he laid out
on top of her. He kissed her and trailed his
tongue over her breast again. Up her chest,
and her neck to her ear. She was breathing
heavy; this made him more excited as he
positioned himself for entry. With great

restraint Black glided himself into her. She was wet and ready for him. He took his time for as long as he could wait. But her breath was coming faster and knew it was time. With one last push that put them both over the edge they climaxed in perfect unison.   They lay there, spent and sated. Black held her in his arms till they both fell asleep.

The next morning brought good byes, from the parents as they headed back to their estate. They promised to return regularly for visits. Victoria cried at the sight of her parents leaving. Black put his arms around her to assure her they would be back and soon.

That night Black had a special night planed for his new bride. It was a warm so he took her out on the grass with a blanket and they laid their and watched the stars until Victoria was almost asleep. Another experience to check off.

Doc returned a few weeks later. He was sorry to have missed the weddings but he figured Victoria's life was more important. It took him a while to locate his friend and get some information from him. All thought this alternative way of birthing isn't the safest it's the only chance she has. Doc's friend talked him through the procedure. However with it mothers have a tendency to bleed out. And infection was high with this surgery. But it was something he thought. Him and Black went over the plan for the delivery. Black was still unsure about this whole process. But it was what it was.

The days and weeks went by as Black tried to give Victoria every experience he could think of. He did put a stop to her horse riding as she grew bigger. They spent a lot of time doing trivial things around the house. Victory was becoming larger it seemed every day. When Doc said she was about a month away from her delivery. It was time to present Victoria with a present that Black had made for the baby. A cradle with B carved in it. It was beautiful, Victoria loved it and had it placed next to their bed.

One night Black decided to have a midnight snack. The two sneaked down the back stairs to the kitchen. Black went down

first in front of Victoria in case she slipped.

 She was getting big enough now that she

was clumsy. But God Black thought she was

so beautiful even with her rounding belly.

 Black jumped the last step and spun

around to help Victoria down the last steps.

As he turned around their was loud whack

and everything instantly went black for

Black.

Victoria let out a scream quickly her

mouth was covered with a rag. She went

down quickly with the laced clothe. The

perpetrators left as quickly as they came.

Hours later Black came to as the first

lights of day came thru the windows in the

kitchen.   He got himself up and

staggered to a nearby stool. As he looked down he saw a large board. Then it hit him he was hit Victoria! "Victoria!" He screamed, "Victoria" His heart sank and fear griped him. 'Victoria" Within minutes Doc entered the kitchen. He ran straight to Black and righted him on the stool. Tristan and Dirk came running in while Doc ripped his night shirt and pressed it to Blacks cut on his head. Black started to talk a mile a minute. Black waved off Doc assistance. Tristan, Dirk we need to gather the men quickly. He turned to Doc in a panic they took her damn it they took her Doc. Black jumped up and started pacing, just then Richard came barging in the kitchen door. "I saw them Black the bastards who took Victoria!" Black cleared the space between them quickly. "What? speak up man what did you see, tell me what you found man!"

Richard was still trying to catch his breath. He explained that he was out checking on the foul that was born yesterday afternoon. "I was coming out of the barn when I heard voices, men that I didn't recognize so I fell back and followed them. By the time I got up to the kitchen they were already coming out with Victoria. So I followed soon as they rode off I took the first horse in the barn and followed. Black they went to the estate just south of here." Blacks hands turned into fist as he swiped out and punched the door next to him. Just then Mary stepped in the kitchen in a frantic. "What's going on, what's happened?" Black spun on his heels to face her, "He took her that bastard." "Who took her?" You can hear the fear rising in Mary as she started to shed tears.

Black turned to Doc, "Doc it was Hans after all, that bastard has her. It was him all along!" Just then the other men all arrived at the house. Black barked out orders and everyone dispersed to fulfill their given orders. Black ran to his room and donned his clothes. As he turned Mary was standing in the door way. "Bring her back Lord Black, Please bring her back." Black gave Mary a hug, "your damn right I will get her back, and the bastard will pay I can guarantee that." Black was beyond mad he in a state of madness, and Mary knew this man Hans will rue the day he was born by the time her brother gets done with him.

The men set out with Doc in tow. After a few miles Black gave the order to dismount in a group of trees near the estate. They walked the rest of the way. As they hid in the tree line surrounding the estate Black worked out a plan. They split up and get inside threw all directions. If someone was found out the others still had a chance. With that they broke and headed off into different directions. Black and Doc stay put for a moment. Just as Black was about to leave Doc stopped him. Black hunkered back down so Doc can say his peace. "Black I will be right here and will wait. You need to get Victoria to me as quickly as possible. In her state there's no telling what can happen." Black nodded to Doc and slipped off into the darkness.

Her head was swimming in pain. She was having a hard time focusing on her surroundings. She didn't know what happened and couldn't make since of anything. "It's the chloroform my dear precious angel." Victoria stiffened, "oh God, No please no." So you thought you could just leave us behind did you? Well your home now and you will have to pay for your little vacation. I see that you brought me a present." Victoria quickly took in her surroundings to find she was on the table. Man's table that he used to experiment on her. She was tied down and couldn't move. "Well I guess your home coming will be short lived since you will be our next offering. It was so nice of Lord Black to provide us with pregnant whore, this way we don't have to go find one.

Man started to cut her clothing away. She was only in a night shirt and he made short work of it. He used a knife and every so often he would nick her skin and draw blood. A pain started deep inside her. She wanted to draw her legs up with the pain but her training thru the years taught her to lay still and quiet and it won't hurt as bad. Man left the room and he didn't return for some time. A women came in and started to clean Victoria's naked body. The girl didn't talk, she knew she wouldn't, you're not allowed to talk here. The girl felt Victoria's belly down low at the same time as a contractions hit. Victoria was starting to panic. She knew what was coming, what

the offering was. The girl knew that
Victoria was in labor and she left, left her
their alone in the office.

About an hour later Victoria was in full
blown labor. Man walked in and seemed
very pleased with himself. "Ahh I see I
taught you well my angel." He wiped the
table between her legs and held up his hand
to show her the blood. Victoria panicked
she had to get to Doc he could save the
baby. "My God women you are beautiful
pregnant it's a shame to see it go to waist.
But you know the routine and how this
works. But this time unlucky for you, you
will be the one." With that he cut her
bonds and a young naked boy walked in and
tied her hands in front of her. "Get up my
lovely it's time to pay the piper. Don't

worry I won't make this quick or painless."

 As they were leaving the room Man pulled her hair back snapping her head backwards. "you were supposed to be mine you little bitch. It was me who kept you alive all these years away from everyone else. I owned you and kept you alive and this is how you repay me? By getting knocked up by that bastard Black? Well now it will be over soon and a new one will take your place. You see you are as disposable as the shit in a drain." With that he let her go and led her to the offering hall. The room was full of people. A huge table was set with lots of food. Everyone wore masks and hoods. The room was filled with men and women. Where in this house they would come to live out fantasies. Even now as they walk by the drunken pile of people they were taking the naked servants and either doing things to them or having them do things to them.

Vile raised up in Victoria's throat as she saw the lude acts happening. Finally they made it to the altar. Naked and in pain Victoria was made to lie on the alter table. Man left her there so that her labor could progress for all to see. She was bleeding she could feel it. It was running down her leg when she was walking. Her bindings were cut again as four naked servants held her down. The pain was getting worse and she almost couldn't stand it anymore. She laid their sprawled out naked with her arms and legs held by children.

Black climbed the ivy outside the side window. There was a balcony he was hoping to find an open door or window. He was in luck the door was open he made his way into the room and could hear the sound of people laughing and enjoying themselves. Black heard a noise and duct into a cove in the hall way. He peered out to see it was Cron and Tristan they had made it in also. Just as Black was going to rally them some servants came down the hall. Black was disgusted they were but children. They were naked and had neck collars on.

As soon as they passed Black gave the order and they stealthy went down the hall to the stairs. The place was massive, and dark. All the rooms that lined the hallway were closed. They made their way down the stairs to the grand hall. The doors were closed, they were very large and Black tried to think of a way in without people noticing. But he didn't know what was on the other side. So the men silently broke up to find another rout in. Black came to a room on the side, it was dark so he left the door ajar so he could see when his eyes adjusted.

 But when they did he was horrified to find a small room crammed with little naked bodies. There must have been a dozen children in their all sitting and huddled together. Black froze at the horrible sight. Just then Cron silently entered the room. He too was disgusted with what he saw.

"Tristan found a way around the other side that has a back corridor into the room." Black nodded and gave Cron the word to get the children out of the house. He nodded his understanding as Black caught up with Tristan. They hunkered down to make a plan but Tristan spoke up. "Black I went to the end of the hall and close to it is an altar. They have Victoria on this alter, she is naked and there's a lot of blood. Black nodded and told Tristan to help Cron get the children out and search the house for anymore. He nodded and headed back that way. Black just about jumped out of his skin with fury seeing Victoria laying their on that alter. Just then Dirk showed up. Black ordered him to start a large fire in a room near the great hall.

Dirk ran to do his bidding knowing time was of the essence.

Man stepped up to the alter with a dagger in hand. Victoria was close to the peak of her labor now and that's when Man liked to do the offering. He lifted the dagger and mumbled some words. He brought the dagger to Victoria's belly.

Black was horrified as he realized the offering wasn't Victoria but the unborn child, *their* unborn child. With that fear welling up inside of him he jumped out and tackled the man with the dagger, not only knocking him down but out. People started screaming and running for it. As they opened the doors to the great hall smoke filled the room. These people were not fighters; they have identities that they didn't want anyone to see. So they ran.

Black grabbed Victoria off the table as Richard came in. He grabbed a discarded robe and handed it to Black who wrapped up Victoria. "How is she doing?" Richard asked concern written all over his face. "Not good we need to get her to Doc and home quickly." Just then Hans went running by, Richard jumped up to give chase. Black held Victoria she was losing to much blood he started to pick her up and she cried out in pain. He set her back down; his own clothing was coved in her blood now. Victoria faintly reached up and grabbed Blacks shirt. Black looked down at her, he was beginning to panic. She touched him, ran her palm along his face and gave him a week smile. "Black, save our baby she said." With that he lost her, she fainted. Unconscious Black grabbed her up and started running for Doc. By the time he arrived at the edge of the field the house was in flames. Doc was no were to be found. Black panicked, "stay with Victoria Stay with me don't you dare leave me." With that Doc show up, he had gone to the barn and commandeered a small horse and cart. Black just looked at him in surprise, "that's right I have a few tricks left up these sleeves." Doc gave Victoria a quick look then snapped orders out to black. "Drive Black, drive for home like the devil himself is after you." Black turned and jumped on the pony and pushed it to a go as fast as its little legs would carry it.

When they reached the house Mary came running out. Doc jumped down off the cart and barked orders to Mary who ran back inside to do his bidding. Black ran to the back of the cart and picked up Victoria's limp body, "we're losing her Black quickly to the room.

As they reached the room Black laid her on the bed that Mary was stripping the blankets off. He unwrapped her and Doc took over. He looked her over an gave Black a bleak look. I can't do the surgery, She has lost to much blood already." Just then Victoria came to. Weakly she reached out for Black. "save the baby, it's too late for me you must save our child". Black shook his head, "no Doc will fix it, won't you Doc." If I take the baby she will die" If you don't take it she will die" Do it Doc get it

out of her, she is strong she will make it she

has to make it." With that the door opened

and Dirk ran in. "Take Black out of here I

don't care if you have to knock him out get

him out!" Doc shouted. "Black I will do

what I can for her I promise." With that he

was lead from the room by Dirk. It was

only minutes later that a maid brought out

sheets they were covered in blood. Black

jumped up and ran into the room Dirk hot

on his heels. He grabbed Black by the

shoulders and they wrestled to the ground.

But Black regained his footing first and

made it to the bed. He jumped on the bed

next to Victoria. "I'm staying Doc don't try

to get me out of here it will only get

someone hurt", he said as he looked at

Dirk. Doc nodded and Dirk left the room.

"Well if you insist on being in here you

might as well help. Now listen to me very

carefully Black we only have one shot at

this." Black nodded he would do anything

to save her. Victoria opened her eyes and

looked at Black. She was full of sweat and

had blood splattered on her face. She

managed a weak smile. Black tried to smile

back but he couldn't. "Stay with me

Victoria, Don't you give up on me." She

gave him a weaker smile, closed her eyes

and went limp. Doc listened to her chest.

There was no sound. Doc grabbed his bag

and swung it open. He reached in and

pulled out the scalpel. He cut into her

abdomen and with a gush he punched the

sack. He reached in and after a few seconds

pulled out a lifeless little body. He handed the baby off to the nurse maid. Doc quickly closed the wound. Black was in shock.

He stared at her willing her to move, to breath. He jumped up on his knees and took her head in his arms and screamed at her, "breath damn it, breath!" he yelled at her. He shook her and yelled, pleading for her to come back. He broke down and started to cry, it couldn't end this way it just couldn't. He looked at Doc and pleaded for him to do something. Doc just solemnly shook his head. "She's gone Black I'm sorry we tried. It's what she wanted."

Black threw himself off the bed and start screaming and crying, "No, no I won't let her go!" He walked back to the bed and stared down at his beloveds lifeless body. Tears flowing unchecked. Then to everyone's surprise Black jumped on the Bed and picked Victoria up and slapped her, "wake up damn it you, wake up" He slapped her again "Come on woman you are stronger then this wake up!" He held her close and cried. A cry of a man being ripped apart. Doc put his hand on Black, "come on son there's nothing more we can do." Black just held her and held her tight. With his free hand he started to straighten the blood soaked sheets around her. Acting almost like a man with madness. But he held her and held her.

Blacks sobs caught in his throat as he felt a tinny hand slightly squeeze his arm. He looked down to see two beautiful green eyes staring at him. She was pale, but she was alive. Doc rushed in and grabbed her hand checking for a pulse, and he found one. Black gently laid her on the bed as Doc checked her. Her heart was weak but it was beating. Black grabbed a pillow and put it under her head. Mary ran to get fresh bedding. Black was kneeling next to the bed holding her hand and crying. She made it.

Doc tapped Blacks shoulder. "Come son let her rest now, she's had a tough go of it." Black kissed the hand he was still holding. They had cleaned the bed up and got a fresh night shirt on her. Mary looked at

Black, "Brother why don't you go get some rest, I will watch her for a while." Black nodded, he was spent. He walked out of the room to a hallway of men, his men. They all looked at him expectantly. Black hit the first chair he came to and sank into it, putting his head down and his head between his hands he cried. This time a happy cry.

CHAPTER 9

Victoria went in and out of consciousness for a few days. Doc kept a close eye on her for infection or any unordinary bleeding. After a few days of worrying with her having fever and some vomiting she seemed to pull though. Although she was very week she sat up in bed and ate a bit then asked for her baby. She looked from Black to Doc as if waiting for permission. Then she saw a sad look in their eyes. Victoria started to panic, did her baby not make it? Where was her child? Just then Lord and Lady Holloway and Richard and Mary entered the room. Lady Holloway held in her arms her baby wrapped up in a blanket. Victoria's parents eyes looked tired and sunken. Victoria panicked and in her panic her mother gently laid the bundle in her arms with tears in her eyes.

Black sat next to Victoria on the bed as she moved the blanket to see her child's face. She was beautiful, dark hair, tinny fingers, ears and nose. Black kissed her on the head then kissed his daughters head.

Black then looked at Victoria and asked to please not wake the babe because she was a screamer. They had all been taking turns taking care of her but she never stopped crying for her mother.

Victoria laughed, that's why everyone was so solume, they were warn out taking care of them. Black kissed her on her head and lovingly said, "this babe is a fighter and as strong as her beautiful mother".

With that the room emptied so the couple could enjoy their new baby. Victoria looked at her beautiful baby and then at her beautiful husband. "Life is perfect she peacefully thought to herself".

Epilogue

Huns Vouthschmiit was executed by the Queen. Black, Victoria, Mary and Richard came to London a week before the execution.

The first night in London Black left Victoria, Mary and Baby Sophia with her parents. It was time he confronted the MAN!

Black spent a few hours with Huns, in the end he had the names of prominent members of this satanic group. Victoria begged her husband to take her to see the Man. Finally the night before the execution when Hans was moved to the lower cleaner room of the tower to await his moment with the reaper, Black caved and took Victoria.

Late that evening Black and his men, including his new brother in law escorted Victoria to the tower. Nobody really understood why she wanted to go but Black had an idea that she needed to put and end to this part of her life.

The men held back a few feet from the door as Black walked her up to the little window. He opened it and glanced inside. Gave the ok and the guard opened the door. Victoria stepped inside with Black and the guard following behind.

Victoria saw the once proud man now chained to the was and sitting on the floor like a dog. Victoria looked at him and almost had some pity for him. That quickly changed as he looked up at her and smirked a disgusting smile at her.

"Oh the whore came to say goodbye to her Master"? Black restrained himself from killing the man then and there. Victoria suddenly looked at him and walked close to his ear and placed a replica crucifix of the one in her beloved chapel on his lap and said, "I am sorry that you will never know my true Master"! With that she turned, smiled at Black and walked out the door.

ABOUT THE AUTHOR

Victoria Southard is a proud mother of three boys and one girl along with one in heaven. Married for 26 years to the love of her life. She has an Associates in Teaching, Booking Certificate, along with a Certificate in Hospitality. She is an avid reader and crafter. Vicki loves to write along with sewing, paper crafting and crocheting.

None of her stories have been not been professionally edited and are in hard form.